Orphans of the Night

~~~~~~~~~~~

Orphans of the Night

~~~~~~~~~~~~~~~~~~~~~~

edited by

Josepha

Sherman

walker and company
new york

First published in the United States of America in 1995 by Walker Publishing Company, Inc.

Published simultaneously in Canada by Thomas Allen & Son Canada, Limited, Markham, Ontario

Library of Congress Cataloging-in-Publication Data
Orphans of the night / edited by Josepha Sherman.
p.   cm.
Summary: Includes thirteen stories, written by such authors as Mike Resnick, Pamela Service, Harry Turtledove, and Susan Shwartz, about strange, eerie, and bizarre creatures from the universe of folklore.
ISBN 0-8027-8368-6
1. Children's stories, American.   [1. Animals, Mythical—Fiction.
2. Short stories.]   I. Sherman, Josepha.
PZ5.0695   1995
[Fic]—dc20   95-972
CIP   AC

Book design by Ron Monteleone

Printed in the United States of America

2   4   6   8   10   9   7   5   3   1

Contents

~~~~~~~~~~~~~

Introduction

Josepha Sherman

~~~~~~~~~~~~~~~

Welcome to the world of the strange, the eerie, the unfamiliar, and the wonderfully bizarre. In short, welcome to the world of the Orphans of the Night. Here you will find no clichéd vampires, no trite and toothless werewolves. Orphans of the Night are those creatures out of the universe of folklore who are all around us but are seldom seen—and never by daylight. They roam in every corner of the world, from our own Northwest Coast to the endless desert wastes of Mongolia—to the space just behind your back. Sometimes terrifying, sometimes deadly, but always fascinating, the Orphans of the Night lurk just out of sight in the depths of the forest or the sea or in the recesses of our own dreams.

But now some of those dreams have been brought into the world of the waking by the talented, award-winning writers of this all-new, all-original collection of fantasy stories. They have dared to tell the tales.

Do you dare to read what they have written? Do you dare to enter the world of the Orphans of the Night?

Orphans of the Night

~~~~~~~~~~

Squonk-ing

~~~~~~

Mike Resnick and

Nicholas A.

DiChario

My sister, Meg, isn't exactly a beauty queen, but she's got no reason to cry in front of the bathroom mirror. This is the second time this week I catch her. Girls are given to weird moods, but this is ridiculous.

"What exactly is wiggling up your butt lately?" I ask her. I can't let her think I care or anything, but I'm a little worried about her anyway.

She glances at me in the mirror. Her eyes are red and puffy. Her skin is awful white, too.

"What do you care?" she says.

She should be mad as hell at me for butting into her private bathroom time, but she just rinses out her toothbrush and puts it back in the cup on the sink.

"When's the last time you used your hairbrush? Your hair looks like crap," I tell her.

"You have no sensitivity," she says, and turns around and walks right past me without looking. "Go suck dirt."

1

No sensitivity? *Of course* I have no sensitivity. But go suck dirt? Any guy who would let his older sister talk to him like that without at least a kick-and-run would be laughed clear out of Pennsylvania by the other guys, but since no other guys are hanging around the house today—Mom and Dad won't allow it anymore without "special permission," which I haven't gotten since Pauly and I hung Meg's goldfish from the clothesline to see if it would dry—I decide to let the insult pass. Something strange is going on with that girl, and I'm going to find out what it is.

~

Angela is the most beautiful girl in the whole neighborhood and the whole school, and it is my good fortune that Meg is her best friend. I know all the guys are jealous, but they can't say anything about it because it's not cool to like girls. But whenever Angela is at our house, I always draw a crowd.

The two of them will usually talk a thousand miles an hour right over each other about what this guy said or what this girl did to her best friend—you can never follow exactly what they're saying—and us guys always try to play football or soccer or something in the yard, in full view of the girls. But today I park my butt in the living room chair, where Dad usually sits, and I pretend to read the newspaper. (Dad had to go to the office this morning or he'd be here reading the local business page.) I'm not much of a reader, but I think Angela likes brains.

Today, though, both Meg and Angela are just sitting in front of the TV like a couple of lumps, not even really paying any attention to MTV. Every so often they'll sigh or snap gum. At one point Meg says, "I can't believe all of those starving children in Africa, and the government won't do anything about it."

"We are a country of barbarians," says Angela.

Meg nods sadly. "I know. We've got drug lords pushing to kids, gang members killing each other. And the child abuse . . . dear God . . . it's enough to . . . to make you cry." She sniffles.

I lower the newspaper and stare at them. "All right, what's bugging you two? Who died?"

"Don't mind Alfred," says Meg. "He's got the attention span of a snail, and a personality to match. He'll go away after a while."

Alfred? Yeah, it's my name, all right. But I can't remember the last time my sister used it. Butt-head, Liver Lips, Mule Breath, Dungeon Worm—she's got all sorts of pet names for me. But Alfred?

"Let's go," says Angela. She hasn't even glanced at me all morning. I thought for sure the newspaper would work. I mean, I'm not that much younger than her—two years, is all.

"Where to?" says Meg.

"The park, I guess. Maybe Karen and Jan are there."

Meg nods and gets up off the couch.

The park? Everybody knows that's a guy thing. Guys go exploring in the woods, go fishing in the creek that runs through the cemetery, bike along the dirt paths that cut through the open fields behind the railroad tracks. But girls? Girls never go to the park. They go to the mall or to the pizza place or to somebody's house and do their hair and their makeup and dance with each other in front of MTV. I wonder what's bothering Meg.

I get up off the chair and watch Meg and Angela walk down the street and disappear behind the Clemsons' house. I think long and hard about squealing on Meg. She's not supposed to go to Hemlock Park without an adult. Mom is across the street helping Mrs. Loberta fill out wedding invitations for her fat daughter's wedding. I could go right over there and drop a line like, "I wonder what Meg and Angela are doing in the park today?" But if I squeal on Meg, Meg will tell Angela I opened my big yap, and that will definitely be a strike against me.

So instead I think about forgetting the whole thing. The "X-Men" are on in twenty minutes. After that I can always bike over to Gary's, where there's no special permission rule. We could get a game of football going. But then I remember what Meg said. She said I had the attention span of a snail. Normally, I wouldn't care about something like that. But last week Mom and Dad balled me out because I wasn't paying attention in class. "No attention span" is exactly what Mr. Dobson told them. Dad made sure to repeat the words to me several times in a row, just to make sure they got through. Something tells me Meg was paying attention, too.

I wouldn't want to prove any of them right. No, I was going to find out what was bothering Meg, and I'm not about to give up on it now.

I toss the newspaper aside and chase after the girls.

～

It's not like they're tough to track. Meg and Angela don't even cut through the woods. They walk up to the main entrance of the park and take the sidewalk that all the old people take. They wander past some of the pavilions and the swing sets, and then they follow the creek to where it breaks off into this grassy area surrounded by hemlock trees. It's a nice spot. Me and the guys usually ignore it, though, because it's not very deep into the park.

Sure enough, Jan and Karen are sitting there, with these dull looks on their faces. I sneak behind a hill and climb up and around behind them, taking it real slow and quiet so they don't hear me. By the time I creep into spying position—I can't see very well, but I can hear just fine—they're heavily into more of this weird talk:

"I can't believe there are so many people in this country living under the poverty level." (That's Jan.)

Long pause.

"I hope the president can do something about it." (Meg, who thinks the president can do everything.)

Another long pause.

"But look at the increase in drive-by shootings. Where does that come from? It's the breakdown of society." (Angela's sweet voice.)

"The economy. It's never going to turn around in time to save the small businessperson." (Karen, who must have been listening to Dad.)

SQUONK.

SQUONK.

What the hell was *that*?

SQUONK.

I decide to crawl up the hill a little bit farther so I can get a better look at the circle of hemlocks. I peek over the crest of the hill, and I'm staring right at it: the weirdest-looking animal I've ever seen. Real short, with a body shaped kind of like a penguin's, tiny forepaws, a big head, and round, glistening eyes. But the weirdest thing about it is its ugly skin. From here, it looks as if it's covered head to toe with these really gross dark-brown moles and reddish warts. The animal is sitting up on its haunches right between Meg and a huge hemlock tree. The girls don't seem bothered by it at all.

"SQUONK," it says, a pitiful cry, as if it wants to be included in their boring conversation.

And then I remember something Mr. Dobson said in class about a creature that's rumored to live in the hemlock forests of Pennsylvania. I can't remember exactly what he said about it because I wasn't paying close attention, but he said something about mythology or folklore, I think, and he called the beast a—

SQUONK!

A Squonk! Yeah, he called it a—

SQUONK!

~

That night, after dinner, I ask Dad if I can use his CD-ROM ency-clopedia. Mom and Dad pass this look like they can't believe their ears. Meg is still pushing the food around her plate.

"Sure," says Dad. "The CD is already in. Do you remember how to work it?"

"Sure," I tell him, even though I'm not so sure, but I've just scored a couple of points—one for asking permission to use Dad's computer equipment, and the other for actually wanting to read an encyclopedia—so I'll mess with it till I find what I need.

"Good," says Mom. "Your father and I want to talk to your sister about what's been bothering her."

Normally that'd be a conversation I'd want to spy on, but something tells me they're not going to get anything out of Meg, so I head for the computer in the den.

The encyclopedia is easy enough to use, and I kind of remember how to get around in it. After a few minutes I find exactly what I'm looking for:

"The Squonk," says the encyclopedia in a scratchy voice, "or *Lacrimacopus dissolvens,* is a mythological beast said to be common to the hemlock forests of Pennsylvania. An ugly creature covered with warts and moles, the Squonk is a typically de-pressed little fellow who will often sit in the same place for hours or days, crying unhappily over its own hideous appearance. Too much time spent in the company of a Squonk may lead to a chronic condition known as 'squonking,' in which one will dwell on and complain about current events to the point where melan-cholia or serious depression might set in."

The computer shows me a picture of a penguin-shaped ani-mal just like the one I saw in the park, with brown and reddish splotches all over it, and big, sad eyes, and a drooping face. That's the one, all right. And judging from the behavior of Meg and her friends, they've spent way too much time in its company.

"The Squonk is named after the sound it makes," says the computer, " 'SQUONK, SQUONK,' and can be easily captured in a large bag or sack. However—"

The encyclopedia stops talking. It has reached the end of page one.

A large bag or sack? We've got some potato sacks downstairs in the basement that I'm sure are big enough to hold a squonk. Tomorrow's Sunday. If the girls go to the park, and I follow them, and I've got my sack ready, I can snatch the thing and make a run for it. I can save all the girls. They'll love me. Angela for sure will notice me. And Meg will owe me big-time. Of course I could just tell Mom and Dad what's wrong with Meg and let them handle it, but then I'd be nothing but a snitch.

The encyclopedia prompts me: "Would you like MORE information, or would you like to EXIT the encyclopedia? Please make a selection."

I figure I've seen and heard all I need to see and hear about the Squonk. I select EXIT, the program shuts down, and I head to the basement to prepare my potato sack.

~

After breakfast Meg tells Mom and Dad she's heading over to hang out with Angela. She doesn't say *where* she's going to hang out, of course, a technicality any kid under the rule of strict parents will try to use whenever possible, which is my cue to follow. I grab my sack and trail her to the park, far enough behind so she won't spot me if she happens to glance back.

Meg's friends are already there, sitting on the grass between the hemlock trees, as if they can't wait to start squonking.

This time I don't take up the same position on the hill. Even though the encyclopedia said it's easy to nab a Squonk, I don't want to take the chance of stumbling, or charging straight across the open grass where the Squonk can see me coming. Instead I take my time maneuvering in from the flank, creeping forward tree by tree, waiting, listening, paying attention to the sound of the wind and the birds and the girls' voices and, every so often, a pathetic "SQUONK."

My plan is simple. When I get close enough to see all the girls, and the Squonk is within range, I'll come running full speed into their circle (I want Angela to see me, of course), cut left, pounce on the Squonk, scoop it up in my sack, and sprint straight ahead, deeper into the woods. Once I run past the hemlocks and reach the pines and the creek, I'll set the grubby little monster free. If he makes a new home that far back, he won't be bothering the girls or anybody else for a long, long time.

Suddenly I'm in the perfect position. My heart is thumping pretty good. My senses are all keyed up—the smell of the hemlocks, the feel of the dirt and grass and pebbles beneath my sneaks. My muscles ache to spring into action. Everything comes into focus.

Usually, the longer I wait, the more nervous I get—at least that's the way it goes at the dentist's office—so I leap forward, break through the hemlocks at a dead run. The girls scream. I cut left, and I'm looking straight at the Squonk and its big wet eyes and wart-covered body, and it lets out this super-high-pitched SQUEEEEEK instead of its usual SQUONK, and I bag it, just like that. It's almost too easy.

One of the girls gives me a swift kick in the butt—Meg! Damn it! I didn't expect resistance, especially from my moron sister. But I lift the critter, and I'm up and running. Karen and Jan try to cut me off, but I'm too quick for them. Fake left, fake right, and I'm through the middle. Emmitt Smith couldn't have done it better. I glance over my shoulder, and I see Angela on her knees, crying. Poor Angela. In a few days she'll be thanking me. But Meg is on my tail. "Idiot! Idiot! Get back here! I'm going to kill you!" She actually keeps up with me pretty good for a while, but then she runs out of breath. She stops and pitches a couple of stones at me, but I'm gone. She doesn't know these woods like I do. There's no catching me now.

As I break through the hemlocks and hit the pines, I notice the bag is leaking water. Potato bags always come with tiny holes in them. But why on earth would the bag be leaking water? I reach the creek, out of breath, heart pounding, kneel down, and quickly open the sack. There's no ugly Squonk in it at all. It's just water and a few bubbles. All the water has just about drained out.

I tip the sack upside down, and the last of the bubbly water trickles onto the stones and pine needles at my knees. Nope. Absolutely no Squonk in there. "What the hell is going on here?" I ask. But nobody is around to answer. I *know* I nabbed that Squonk. I just know it. Suddenly I get this sinking feeling in my gut, that rotten feeling you get when you know you've done something really wrong, but you're not exactly sure what it is.

So I walk home slowly, following the creek back to the cemetery, the cemetery back to the park, the park to the main entrance where the old folks walk, and finally around lunchtime I wander home.

~

The moral of the story? Do you really want to know? It's not exactly pretty. It has to do with what Mr. Dobson and Mom and Dad and even Meg said about my attention span. Well, maybe I'd better tell you, after all—maybe then you won't make the same mistake I made.

That afternoon I went back to Dad's encyclopedia, and I looked up the Squonk entry. This time when I got to the page where the program asked me if I wanted MORE information, or if I would like to EXIT the encyclopedia, I chose MORE.

On that second page, the computer told me in its scratchy

voice, "The Squonk is easily frightened, and if trapped or captured, has been known to dissolve into tears and bubbles."

When I got off the computer, I felt like turning into tears and bubbles myself.

Meg still hasn't spoken to me, other than to tell me only an idiot or a fiend would kill a Squonk. I haven't seen Karen or Jan since that Sunday morning. Angela came over one afternoon just to inform me what an insensitive jerk I am. Only two good things came of the whole thing. One: I actually did save the girls from their squonking. Two: The last parent-teacher meeting Mom and Dad went to, Mr. Dobson told them how much more I seem to be paying attention.

But the Squonk is dead.

I can't fix that.

So I figure when I grow up I'm going to set up a park or a national reserve or something so the Squonks can live in their natural habitat and share their misery, and I'll arrange guided tours by people who know all about Squonks so that if humans want to see them they won't bag them and kill them accidentally, and they won't fall victim to that chronic disease known as squonking.

I figure it's the least I can do for the ugly little things.

I have to stop writing now. Even though there aren't any Squonks around, I think I'm going to cry.

The Squonk—Lacrimacopus dissolvens—*hails from the hemlock forests of Pennsylvania. The creature is an ugly misfit covered with warts and moles. As a result, the Squonk is eternally depressed, and weeps constantly, and when frightened or captured, literally dissolves into tears.*

The Njuggle

~~~~~~

Laura Frankos

Rasmus Harraldsoun shoveled stew into his mouth as fast as he could, so eager was he to head for the boat. His father, Einar, was less enthusiastic about the start of the deep-sea fishing season, with its many dangers and long, grueling hours away from their home in Shetland. Father ate slowly, holding his bowl out to Rasmus's mother for another helping. Mother served him in equally grim silence.

Rasmus's grandfather, Olav Larsen, however, talked loudly and often enough for all of them. "Look at Rasmus eating like there's no tomorrow! So you think you can pull oars on a háf-boat, lad?" "Háf" is the ancient Shetlandic word for the ocean, and Grandfather Olav constantly peppered his conversation with old words and phrases. He talked more of ancient legends than of the real people who lived in the sea town of Norwick. Some, like

11

Cousin Magnus, found Grandfather a bore, but Rasmus liked the old stories.

"I did well enough last year, Grandfather," he said between spoonfuls. "I'm sixteen now and much stronger."

"Aye, your father said you pulled your weight, and your help made all the difference after we lost your brothers, with me laid up all those months. A bad year, that was. I thank God that 1876 has been better."

"May it continue to be," said Mother, whose eyes still filled with tears at the memory of the great storm that took her older sons. Grandfather Olav had nearly joined them and had spent months regaining his health. Rasmus was not surprised that Grandfather Olav was itching to return to the háf at last.

Einar Harraldsoun shoved his bowl aside and drank the rest of his tea. "It's time," he said in a low voice. "The others will be waiting for us."

Rasmus held his tongue, though he knew perfectly well Father was the slow one.

"Run ahead, Rasmus, and get the lines from the shed and into the boat," said Father.

Rasmus gave Mother a quick embrace and a wide smile, hoping to ease those worried lines from her brow. It didn't work. She always worried during the háf-season, and even more after last year's storm.

He pelted down the path to the beach, Grandfather Olav and Father following more slowly. He could see Cousin Magnus at the shed bringing out the baited lines, and Magnus's older brothers, Cousins Donald and Johnny, readying the square sail of the sixern.

Magnus waved him over, a broad grin on his freckled face. "So, Rasmus, Grandfather's ready to join us again? I'm glad he's well, but I'll tell you true: It was restful on my ears not to have him in the sixern with us last year. All those endless tales of trolls and monsters! And whacking my cheek with a wet mitten if ever I uttered an unlucky word at sea. As if it made any difference to the fish what fishermen say! Silly superstitions!"

Rasmus shrugged. "I like Grandfather's stories. They help pass the time. You shouldn't complain or tease him, Magnus; he's an old man, so give him respect."

"Och, aye, that I do," said Magnus, but he did not sound at all respectful. "How mad he was when I put a dead mouse in his fish basket years ago! He swore it would bring bad luck, but it didn't, except to my backside." He grinned impishly as Grandfather Olav and Einar approached. "Welcome back, Grandfather!"

"Thank you, lad. Let's see what the waters hold for us this season." Grandfather knelt on the rocky beach, picked up a stone, and addressed the heavens. "Lord, bring us back safe where this stone came from." He chucked the stone into the bottom of the sixern and climbed in after it, taking his place at one of the six oars that gave the little craft its name.

Einar, Donald, and Johnny said nothing as they followed Grandfather, but Magnus made a face at the old man's lucky stone. When Rasmus was certain Magnus was not watching, he slipped a rock into his pocket and muttered the same prayer. Rasmus approved of Grandfather's ways. Even if they were just superstitions, how could they hurt?

~

To Rasmus's disappointment, Grandfather Olav said little as they rowed thirty miles to the open sea. The old man was pale and perspiring, despite the biting wind. He sighed in relief when Einar signaled for them to stop.

Rasmus handed Grandfather a bottle of water, which he took gratefully. "Ah, that's better! It was a long haul, but I made it! Let's set out the lines."

The six fishermen worked quickly. Though late evening, the sun still shone bright because they were so far north, closer to the Arctic Circle than to London. In a few weeks' time, at the summer solstice, it would be dark for just three or four hours. The Shetlanders made the most of those long, bright nights, fishing for cod, mackerel, and ling.

When the miles of lines were cast, Grandfather shouted to the waves, "Roll, roll, rise, and wait! Nibble, nibble, take the bait!"

Magnus ducked his head so Grandfather Olav wouldn't see him laughing at the charm to increase the catch.

They chewed on oatcakes and drank water, waiting for the fish to begin biting. Grandfather was telling the famous story of the two giants tricked by a mermaid when he stopped abruptly and pointed to the east. "Look there, lads! A Sifan! Haven't seen one in years!"

Rasmus looked east. He thought he saw a dark shape moving through the waves far in the distance. Magnus looked, too, and made another sour face.

"Watch the Sifan carefully, Rasmus," said Grandfather Olav, "for if it jumps out of the water and falls to the left, it means death to the fishes and a good catch for us. But if it jumps to the right, it means death to a man. You can see it has the shape of a coffin. Ah, it's swimming away."

"I can't see a thing," complained Johnny. "My eyes are best for close work."

"Do you really believe in such sea monsters?" asked Magnus, this time not hiding the scorn in his voice.

Donald, who never said much, shrugged, but Johnny nodded. "There's all manner of monsters in the world."

"Are you doubting my word, Grandson?" Grandfather Olav thundered.

"Yes," Magnus said bluntly. "There's no such thing as a Sifan. It's probably just a whale. Sometimes whales jump like that."

Grandfather Olav, instead of arguing, shook his gray head and sighed. "I fear for you, lad. It's folk like you that are easiest fooled by the devil's creatures, because you deny they're there. Beware especially the shape changers, like the Njuggle. You'll fall for its tricks, like my friend Andrew Grott, back when we were lads."

Magnus snorted. "I can't keep all your tales straight, Grandfather. What dreadful beastie is the Njuggle? Will he bite my toes off while I sleep?"

Johnny kicked Magnus in the shins, reminding him he owed Grandfather respect.

Grandfather nodded approvingly to Johnny. "The Njuggle is a freshwater demon. He can take many shapes, most often that of a stick of wood or a handsome pony. While he waits for his victim, he roars in anticipation—a sure sign someone will drown that night, when the Njuggle's powers are strongest."

"What happened to your friend Andrew, Grandfather?" asked Rasmus, though he had heard the story many times.

"We were walking home over the hills in the west, not far from Loch Brekkan, when we suddenly saw a pony where nothing had been a moment before! I was wary, but Andrew ran forward and stroked its mane, saying what a fine beast it was and wondering who owned it. The creature never moved, save to raise its head and look at me. Och, those eyes! They shone with hell's fires, they did!

"I told Andrew to stay away, but he laughed at my fears and jumped on its back. The beast galloped off like a Derby winner, with Andrew clinging to it in terror. It vanished over the hill with him. I followed, but there was nothing I could do: That Njuggle had taken Andrew into the loch and drowned him. They found his body next morning. I've carried a charm against the Njuggle ever since; gave one to Rasmus, too, when he asked me for one."

Clearly unimpressed, Magnus was about to retort when Einar jerked a thumb at the lines. "They're biting well. Haul them in fast, and we may have time for a second cast tonight." The dreary work of removing the fish from hundreds of hooks and baiting them again drove away all thoughts of monsters.

~

The háf-season had gone well by late July. The weather was decent and the catches enough to pay the laird his due and then some. Grandfather Olav entertained them with tales of the Stoor Worm, the Fin Folk, the trolls, and the fierce Brigdi, a sea monster so vast he could eat a sixern in one gulp. Even Magnus listened quietly, though sullenly; Rasmus learned Johnny had boxed his ears for his rudeness to Grandfather.

But fortunes change rapidly, as Rasmus's family knew too well. While they were far at sea one night, dark storm clouds began forming in the distance. Not taking any chances, Einar decided to cut the lines and head for home. Donald and Johnny grumbled about his caution, but he snapped, "Better to lose lines than to lose lives."

They rowed like men possessed and beat the storm by a wide margin. Exhausted by the effort, Grandfather Olav coughed and wheezed his way to the croft. Mother was alarmed at their early and empty-handed return but quickly bundled the old man into bed. She searched the kitchen in vain for the cough elixir.

"Rasmus, be a good lad and run over to Auntie Sinnie's for some medicine for that cough, or he'll get no rest tonight."

Rasmus yearned for his bed but did as she asked. Auntie Sinnie's croft was seven miles inland, past the "bachelors' croft" where his three cousins lived. Magnus threw open the door as Rasmus strode by. "Where you off to this hour, Ras?"

"Auntie Sinnie's, for cough liquor."

"I'll come with you," Magnus offered. "I pulled my back rowing and can't sleep. All that hurry, and it's barely drizzling!"

"Aye, but who knows how much rain is falling out at sea?" Rasmus defended his father's decision to turn back early.

As if to prove his point, the rain began pelting down. Magnus grimaced at the sky. Thunder boomed in the distance, followed by a deep roar. The winds playing over the sea caves sometimes sounded like that, but those were miles away. Rasmus thought it peculiar, but Magnus ignored it, pulling his hood over his head. The two young men walked in silence, using Rasmus's lantern to guide their feet.

"Must be around nine o'clock," said Magnus. "Just about sundown, though the clouds are so thick, you'd never know it."

Rasmus nodded, his eyes looking ahead to where the path broadened into the road that led to Loch Brekkan. There was something long and white at the side of the road—a piece of driftwood, he thought. Then his boot caught in the mud, distracting him.

Magnus suddenly exclaimed, "Well, look there!"

Rasmus glanced up from his boot, and there, where he thought he had seen the driftwood, was a dark brown pony, its coat glistening in the rain. Grandfather Olav's story of the Njuggle flashed through his mind. "Don't go near it, Magnus!" he shouted, his throat tightening with fear. Of itself, his hand crept into his coat and reassuringly touched Grandfather's charm.

His cousin stared at him in surprise. "Whatever's the matter? He's a fine gentle pony and doesn't deserve to be left in the rain. We may get a reward for finding him, and if no one claims him, we've a grand little animal for ourselves. Hello, fella! What are you doing out in the wet?" He patted the pony's flanks and walked all around him, admiring. "A good strong back, no marks of ill-treatment. A bit thin, perhaps."

"Magnus, listen," Rasmus pleaded. "Do you remember Grandfather's story of the Njuggle? Just before we saw the pony, I saw a piece of wood lying there. And earlier, I heard a roar or a bellow."

"What of it?" Magnus stroked the pony, which stood calmly in the driving rain. "You're not thinking this splendid little fellow is some weird water demon? Ras, you're getting as daft as Grandfather!"

"He's not daft! Some of his notions are a bit odd. . . ." Rasmus's voice trailed off. It did seem a ridiculous story. The lantern light flickered on a perfectly ordinary-looking pony. Rasmus kicked at the ground. "Maybe we should wait until daylight, or else use this charm Grandfather gave me."

"Ah, you're a frightened baby, just like him. I'm not afraid of this pony!" Magnus vaulted onto its back as a bolt of lightning ripped across the sky. At once, the creature sprang forward, its eyes wide and glowing eerily, its long tail whirling in a circle like a windmill. A peal of thunder nearly drowned out Magnus's terrified scream. The Njuggle galloped down the road some fifty feet, then stopped and tossed its head, taunting Rasmus. It howled triumphantly, knowing it had outwitted a man who recognized it.

"Jump, Magnus!" Rasmus yelled, but Magnus couldn't let go. Rasmus was too far away to pull his cousin from the Njuggle's back, too far to use the charm Grandfather Olav had given him. In rage, he heaved the lucky stone he'd carried all háf-season at the monster. It bounced off the Njuggle's hindquarters, a poor throw that would have barely bruised an ordinary horse. But the lucky stone pained the Njuggle like a hornet's sting. It bucked and for a moment lost its power over Magnus, who fell heavily to the ground and scrambled off the road toward the safety of a stone wall. The Njuggle looked at him. Its eyes were peaceful and dark once more, its ears pricked forward, its posture friendly, not menacing.

Rasmus grabbed the lantern and ran to Magnus's side. The other youth was bruised but not badly hurt.

"Well, Cousin," Magnus gasped, "I admit when I'm wrong: That's no horse. Hey! Keep away from it, Ras!"

Rasmus cautiously approached the monster, Grandfather's charm tightly bundled in his hand. "We've got to capture it, so it won't kill again. After Grandfather's friend drowned, he always carried this with him for protection." He uncoiled a lasso of thin, plaited rawhide, decorated on both sides with small iron studs.

Magnus snorted. "It's too thin to hold him. He may look small, but there's more power in those bones than in any beast I've ever ridden." He shuddered at the memory of the brief ride. "You can't make him come with you using that puny thing."

"It's strong enough because of those studs. Grandfather taught me demons hate one thing: iron. Let's see how the Njuggle likes it!" He tossed the lasso over the monster's neck and braced himself for the reaction.

The Njuggle once again went from gentle pony to a wild-eyed creature of evil. It shied away from Rasmus, bellowing in fury, then halted abruptly when it pulled against the rawhide rope. It threw back its head and screamed in pain. In the faint light of the lantern, Rasmus could see a clear, slimy liquid oozing from sores where the iron studs touched the njuggle's flesh. Rasmus stood his ground, holding firm to his end of the rope. The Njuggle strained and screamed, realizing it was helpless against the iron. Its tail whirled round and round, creating more wind than the storm.

Magnus leaped up to help Rasmus. "I never would have believed it! We've got it! But what do we do with it?"

"The standing stones by Nilsen's beach. It's but another mile, and there are good, stout chains anchored to the stones. Iron chains," Rasmus added.

The mile to the standing stones (which Grandfather Olav claimed were placed there by feuding giants, who tossed them at each other) took nearly an hour to travel. The Njuggle fought every inch of the way, sometimes trying to bite or kick, but always yielding when they pulled on the rope and the studs burned its monstrous flesh.

"Why doesn't it turn back into a stick or something?" Magnus gasped as they tied the lasso to the heavy chains of the stones. "Then it could get away from us."

"Must be the iron," Rasmus said. "Grandfather would know."

"Aye, that he would," said Magnus, with a new note of respect in his voice.

The job done, they stepped away from the creature. The rain tapered off; the moon broke through the clouds, though the wind still blew fiercely. The Njuggle tugged at the rope again, clanking the chains. It glanced toward the east, something like desperation filling its luminous eyes. It pulled harder, ignoring the wounds made by the iron.

"Maybe we should go home before it breaks loose," Magnus said. "It won't be very pleased with us, you know."

Rasmus watched the monster struggle. "Grandfather said its powers were greatest at night. I think it's afraid of being chained when the sun rises. I wish I could stay to see what happens, but I must get that cough liquor to Mother. She'll be worrying after me."

As they hurried back to the road, they could still hear the chains clanking and the Njuggle snorting in frustration. They did not tell Auntie Sinnie of their encounter with the demon; she was too sleepy to understand anything more than that they needed the medicine for Grandfather.

In their haste to return, they did not go back to Nilsen's beach but headed straight for their homes. Magnus paused before entering his croft. "Rasmus, if you don't mind, I'd like to tell Grandfather Olav about the Njuggle myself. I think I owe him an apology."

Rasmus nodded and hurried home to find everyone asleep—Grandfather's cough had quieted without the medicine. He pulled on some dry clothes and staggered into his own cot but soon found he was too tense to sleep; his memory kept reliving the encounter with the Njuggle. He tossed and turned until the faint glow of dawn appeared in his window. He could wait no longer. He had to find out what had happened to the monster. He crept out of bed, grabbed his coat, and went outside.

A brisk wind was blowing in a clear sky as he approached the beach, but all was silent save the pounding of the surf and the cries of the seabirds. Had the Njuggle escaped? As he drew closer, he saw the chains hanging limp and empty, and his heart fell. He ran to the boulders for a better look. The stones were chipped and scarred in many places where the Njuggle had thrashed against the iron that bound him. Shimmering gobs of slime showed where the demon had bled in its efforts to escape.

Crestfallen, Rasmus began to walk back home when a shout came from the west. Magnus ran toward him, crowing gleefully, twirling his hat in his hand in a motion that reminded Rasmus of the Njuggle's whirligig tail.

"Stop your cheering," Rasmus said. "It got away."

"It did not! Come see! I thought the same as you when I got here not long after dawn, but then I found its trail." Magnus grabbed Rasmus by the arm and led him off the gravel beach. "You can see it better on the grass. I think it was trying to get back to its home in the loch; at least, it was headed west when it died."

A few yards up the muddy and grassy slope, Magnus pointed out the demon's spoor: more of the transparent, gooey slime that Rasmus had seen smeared on the standing stones. "Like the world's biggest slug trail," Magnus said. "Follow it for a few paces, Ras, but don't touch it. It burns the skin."

Rasmus did, and once again he met the Njuggle—or what

was left of it. Tangled in the rawhide rope was a gelatinous blob, something like a jellyfish but much larger.

Magnus poked it with a stick. It didn't move. "It's well and truly gone, Rasmus. There's less of it now than there was ten minutes ago. You can see it shriveling up under the sun."

The two young men stood together and watched the Njuggle disappear, never to claim another victim in its loch. "I'll have to get another rope with those iron studs," Rasmus said.

"I want one, too," Magnus said.

~

That night, the fishing was extremely good, and the baskets were full of mackerel and ling. Grandfather Olav was in a jovial mood, never stopping his tale telling while they hauled in the heavy lines. Rasmus and Johnny, as usual, were his most interested listeners, but Grandfather Olav noticed a new attentiveness in Magnus.

"By thunder, Magnus, you almost look like you enjoyed that yarn," said Grandfather. "What's got into you, lad?"

Magnus blushed nearly as red as his hair. "Well, Grandfather, it wasn't so much what's got *into* me as what got *under* me." He glanced at his brothers, who were looking at him curiously, and at Rasmus, who was trying not to laugh. "If you don't mind too much, I'll tell you about it later."

The Njuggle *is a freshwater demon from the Shetland Islands, in far northern Scotland. Most often, it becomes a horse, which then runs into the water, drowning the rider.*

Peeling the Heart

~~~~~~

Jo Clayton

Mercy stood by a pond in the woods and shouted at the moon, "I'm so *tired* of people being kind. I wish they'd just say what they think."

Something stirred in a tree on the far side of the pond. The biggest, blackest bird she'd ever seen hopped from a low branch onto an old refrigerator someone had dumped there after pulling the door off. It perched on one end, eyes glowing like fox fire in rotten wood; then it cawed at her, and in that rusty, creaking sound she thought she heard words: *You don't like this world, try another.*

It flapped its wings and labored up off the refrigerator, moving easier and easier as it rose. Its shadow cut across the round, bland face of the moon, and then it was gone.

Mercy blinked. "Huh? 'Quoth the Raven, Nevermore.' Except it didn't say 'nevermore.' Am I crazy or what?"

She circled the pond and

inspected the refrigerator, clicked her tongue when she saw the marks from the bird's talons in the scum that had dried on the white surface. "Weird."

She settled beside the marks and sat looking into the water, watching the wind blow the moon's image into bits. The disk re-formed and shattered and re-formed again in a hypnotic rhythm as the moon itself climbed higher in the sky.

This wasn't the first time she'd sneaked out of the house and come here to get away from her father. He fussed over her until she felt as if she couldn't breathe, doing things for her she could do perfectly well for herself. And all the time he had to force himself to look at her. He hid it well, and she hadn't noticed until a year ago, just after the last batch of plastic surgery. She couldn't talk to him; he wouldn't listen when she tried to find the words to tell him that pretending not to notice how she looked just made her feel worse. And he tried to buy friends for her. He wanted her to get away from her books, to talk the way the other kids talked, to pretend she was just like everyone else. He was always taking kids from her classes to special treats—movies, skating, a rock concert once, anything he could think of that they would like. He tried so hard she'd almost come to hate him for it.

Her body a knot of tension and resentment, she scrubbed her hands across her face, hating the lumpy lines of scar tissue and the too-slick flesh between them.

She was fourteen, short and fine boned, with pale blond hair, some of it growing in tufts between the burn scars that mottled the left third of her scalp. Usually she wore a scarf her father tied in a turban for her, but she didn't need to do that here. The burns went down her left side, turning her arm into a knotty arc; she could still get some use from the hand, but she couldn't bend her elbow or straighten the arm.

She lifted her head as she heard a rustle among the weeds where she'd been standing.

A porcupine came trundling into the moonlight. It stopped and rose onto its haunches, its small, neat forepaws crossed above its stomach, its black, beady eyes fixed on her. After a minute it dropped to all fours again and came lumbering around the pond. Before it vanished into the dark, it turned its head and spoke to her. "Hey Scab-face, you sitting around uglying up the night? Get a move on; you got things to do." Then it was gone.

She blinked again, got to her feet. "I better go home. Any more of this, and I'll be thinking my name is Alice and go hunting rabbit holes."

~

The wood was a small triangle of wasteland on the edge of the development where she lived, a mix of half-grown alders and cottonwoods, brush, weeds, discarded trash, and muck; the air had a sour, musty odor from the puddles of stagnant water and the dozen sorts of fungi that grew everywhere.

There was a field on the west side of the triangle where a farmer kept a few riding horses; a highway ran past on the north. Other times when she was coming home after wandering about the dog paths that crisscrossed the wood, she'd hear big trucks rumbling by, the horses stomping and whickering at each other, but tonight was very quiet. She started to get scared and walked faster for a few steps, then stopped.

Burned arm pressed against her ribs, held in place with her good hand, she turned slowly, her eyes widening, her breath coming faster. "My name's not Dorothy either, and for sure I'm not in Kansas anymore. Not that I was to begin with."

A cool breeze with a touch of frost in it stirred the needles of huge pine trees; the path was wider than she remembered, darker, prickly with dry, discarded pine needles. The sour smell was gone, replaced with the clean, acrid scent of the mountains.

"I've read lots of stories like this." Her voice threatened to break; she stopped, started again. "I mean, maybe I'm really back in bed, dreaming." She closed her eyes, sucked her bottom lip between her teeth, and bit down hard. It hurt. It kept hurting when she let it go. "Wake up wake up wake up," she chanted.

When she opened her eyes, she was standing on that path carpeted with dead needles, with those pines rising up and up all around her, awesome as the trees in the redwood forest her parents had taken her to see before the accident.

"Well, I can pull up a piece of dirt and sit here howling or go looking for someone who can tell me where I am and how I can get home." The words sounded brave, and when she finished saying them, she felt better.

Still cradling her arm, her eyes searching the moonlit darkness under the pines for some clue as to where she was, she began walking along the trail.

She walked and walked, and nothing changed, just trees and trees and a path winding along a mountainside.

A while later, she wasn't sure how long it was, she heard a sudden squeal filled with pain and fear, then thrashing noises. Some kind of animal—it sounded as if it was caught in a trap. She liked animals and planned to be a veterinarian, but the wild ones were dangerous: They could hurt her or give her rabies. All those warnings in school . . .

As she hesitated, an otter came from under the trees, crept on its belly toward her, and laid its head on her foot.

It was a beautiful creature, long and sleek with thick, dark fur her fingers itched to stroke, though she didn't dare touch it. Then she wondered if it would talk to her as the porcupine had. "What do you want?"

It didn't speak, just lifted its head and whimpered.

"I'll help if I can. What do you want?"

It switched ends with a swift, sinuous movement and began walking away, heading toward the thrashing and the shrieking, looking back at her again and again.

She followed.

At the edge of a small meadow, near a stream, a much smaller otter was fighting to free himself from a wire snare that had tightened about one of his forelegs just above the paw. When she knelt beside him, he snapped at her, tried to rake his claws across her arm.

She wriggled out of reach, scowled at the older one. "You must be his mother. Can you get him to calm down?"

The other end of the wire was twisted about a root, but it was pulled too tight to let her work the twist loose. "Sit on him," she said. "Hold him down. Hm. I need something to keep him from scratching and biting me."

As the otter stretched herself over her child, Mercy took off one of her loafers, thought a minute, pulled her dress over her head. She managed to trap his muzzle in the shoe, used the dress as more padding, then took a firm hold of the trapped leg with her good hand, lifted it to get some slack, and after what seemed like an eternity managed to loosen the wire enough to pull the noose over his paw.

She flung herself back as the youngster exploded away from his mother and her, leaped into the stream, and crouched on a boulder out in the middle of the water, shaking his leg and keening at the pain. The mama otter splashed out to him and began licking at the wound.

His teeth had ripped apart the upper on her shoe. She took off the other loafer and dropped it beside the ruined one. "Well, baby, you might as well have this one, too; you can use it for a chew toy." Neither otter paid any attention to the sound of her voice. She shrugged and picked up her dress.

It was torn and spattered with the youngster's blood, but she shook it out and put it on because bad as it was, it was better than walking along in her underwear.

"A thank-you would be nice. No? Well, bye." She went back to the path and started walking along it, wincing a little as the needles pricked against the soles of her bare feet.

The trees closed round her again; the sound of the stream was lost in the whisper of the needles. The path wound on and on, and after an endless while she began to wonder if she'd ever get anywhere. She kept walking because there didn't seem to be any point in stopping.

"That was a good thing you did, Mercy."

She wheeled.

Her mother was standing between two pines, smiling at her, just as she remembered her, though her upper lip was drawn up to meet her nose so it looked like an otter's mouth.

"Go away," she said. "You're dead. It isn't fair. Don't do this to me. You're dead."

"Dead is different than you think," her mother said. "I'll walk with you awhile."

Mercy stared at the ground as she walked. Without looking at her mother, she said, "What am I doing here? What is this place?"

"A Kushtaka heard you. Remember the stories I told you when you were hardly to my knee?"

"No. It wasn't you. It was my mother. You're not my mother."

The ghost hummed a tune as she walked, a song Mercy remembered too well. She tried to stop listening, but she couldn't. "Why did you crash the car?" she burst out. "Why did I have to get burned like this? Made a freak no one can look at without getting sick."

The ghost stepped in front of Mercy, stopping her. A misty hand held out a carrot. A silly, ordinary carrot. "Eat this," her mother said. "It's good for you." Her mother was always trying

28

to get her to eat carrots. You want sharp eyes, she'd say, and a carrot's a root, a strong root. It ties you to the earth. You don't want to go floating off, now do you? Mercy the Macy's balloon. They used to laugh when Mercy said that, her mother and her.

She took the carrot and bit off a piece. The ghost vanished at the first crunch of her teeth.

She walked along, chewing on the carrot. When she'd finished all but the end and was getting ready to throw that away, the porcupine came from behind a tree, sat up in the middle of the path. "You don't want that bit; give it to me."

"Porcupines aren't supposed to talk."

"I'm not talking. What? You crazy? Give me that carrot end."

She stared at him a moment, then started giggling. Little snorts of laughter escaping her, she curtsied and bent down, holding the carrot nub on her palm.

He took it in nimble black forepaws, held it between them and nibbled at it, popped the last bit in his mouth, wiped his paws on his belly fur. "You'd better be ready to run," he said. "Or you'll lose your place and get dumped in the ocean. Shark out there likes girls, even tough, scabby ones with no meat on their bones like you."

"What?"

"Mind what I saiiiiiiid. . . ." The last word trailed off in a long scream as everything about her started to race away from her. The scream pinched off. Sound faded.

The mountain and the trees and the path and everything fled from her faster and faster until there was nothing but a blur. Then cold salt water splashed about her ankles, stinging the cuts the needles had made in her feet.

She gasped, cried out, and started running.

Before she'd taken three steps, the rushing stopped, and she found herself on a broad, sandy beach, looking up over a ripple of dunes at jagged mountain peaks with a dusting of snow like white sugar.

Sound came back.

She heard shouting behind her, wheeled. Her mouth dropped open, and her eyes went wide.

A dandelion seed with a cloud of white fluff the size of a semi truck wafted by high overhead. Attached to the oval, black seed like the tail on a kite was a line of people holding onto each other and yelling at her. The last and lowest was a small boy with a coarse thatch of black hair falling into his eyes. One of his hands was free, and he was waving it at her.

When she just stood there staring, he started wailing. Something about him reminded her of the babies in the burn unit; she bent over, vomited everything in her stomach, then splashed sea-water on her face. When she straightened, he was still wailing as he bobbed along just above the water but unable to touch it.

She ran after him, caught hold of his hand. For an instant she felt weightless as that fluff, then she pushed her heels down so they dug into the sand. Rooted and solid, she pulled harder until the boy's feet touched the ground.

He broke loose, then grabbed at the woman next in line. "Mama," he cried. "Mama."

Mercy caught the woman's foot with her good hand and helped the boy haul her down.

One by one, all the people came to ground again, and the seed went drifting on alone.

As soon as the last person touched down—there were a round dozen men, women, and children—they weren't people anymore but ravens, big black birds swirling round her, brushing her with their wings. The touches sent energy coursing through her like the time when she was just two and stuck her finger into a light socket. Not frightening like that had been, though, but wonderful. She wanted them to go on and on. . . .

The whirl of ravens was over in a few seconds. Before she had time to gather herself and ask them to help her as she'd helped them, they were gone, the flock a black smudge flying toward the mountains.

She stood alone on the beach, trying to figure out what she should do next. The moon was low in the west, and she had a feeling that she had to reach a place, she didn't know what place, before the night was over. She started to take a step, nearly fell over. Her foot was caught. Frightened, she jerked harder.

The foot came reluctantly loose from the hollow her heel had dug in the sand. "Like pulling a carrot," she said. "Mama said carrots rooted you to the earth. No, that's silly. It's just my foot. I'm tired and stiff, that's all." She freed her other foot, rubbed at her eyes. "Where's that dumb porcupine when I need him?"

"Hurry, child, we haven't much time left." A woman stood atop a dune looking at her, a long, slim woman with short legs and arms that grew from her chest instead of her shoulders.

"Who're you?"

"Take my hand. Be quick, child."

"My name's Mercy. Don't call me child." She sighed and began trudging up the side of the dune, using the clumps of sea grass to keep from slipping down again.

When she reached the crest, she shied away from the hand the woman held out to her. "You go ahead. I'll follow."

"Take care you don't get lost, Mercy. Don't look away from me whatever happens."

"All right. So let's go."

Mercy's first step was on sand, the next on pine needles, the third on meadow grass, then she was walking with ordinary steps, following the woman across a small meadow with a pond in the middle—a pond that looked like an untrashed copy of the one in the wood by her house. She heard a splash, turned her head, and saw a frog crawling out of the water.

It looked as if something had been chewing on it; it was horribly torn, oozing blood and slime, making little screaming sounds, and seemed so badly hurt it shouldn't be alive. It lifted its head. "What are you staring at, Ugly? Never seen someone dying before? You useless, or are you going to help me?"

"How?" she said. She tried to look away, but she couldn't. The thing was so horrible, it was fascinating.

"Why you asking me? I'm just a frog. You're the one that wants to be a vet."

"But I'm not, and I won't be for years." She took a step backward. He was a nasty creature, angry and full of hate; it blasted out at her, gave her strength to wrench her eyes away from him. She looked for the guide, but the woman was gone. The meadow was empty of life and silent except for the sickening noises from the frog and the soft whispers of the pines. *I'm lost for sure,* she thought. *Stupid to forget what she said. I'll never get out of here now. Maybe . . . maybe I can catch up with her.*

She started for the trees, then something made her look back at the gruesome frog. He had stopped whimpering and was just sitting there at the edge of the water, piteous golden eyes fixed on her, pleading with her. As she gazed at him, it was as if his skin had peeled back to show her his heart, tender and hurting and very afraid.

She went over and squatted down beside him; as carefully and gently as she could, she eased her good hand under him and lifted him from the mud. Though she couldn't help him, maybe she could get him to someone who did know what to do. Trying not to jar him, she got to her feet and took a step toward the trees.

He burst apart messily in her hand, all slime and blood and gobbets of flesh. An instant later a large butterfly stood on her palm, its crumpled wings straightening out, shining white velvet wings with a lacy pattern in black velvet written across them. It worked its black thread legs, flapped its wings, and rose into the air to hover before her face. In something like a kiss it brushed its antennae across her brow, then flew away.

"You're the biggest fool for standing round gawking I ever saw." It was the porcupine again. "They're waiting for you. Get a move on."

She wiped her hand on her dress and grinned at him. "So, lead off. I'll follow."

They turned a corner that wasn't there, and she was in a long, dark room lit by torches burning on the walls. There were a lot of people in the room, some she didn't know, but she thought she saw her mother's ghost a time or two and another of them looked like her father, and three or four more seemed to be kids from school; she couldn't be sure because all of them had otter mouths, and some had their arms growing out of their chests instead of from their shoulders.

One of the men started playing a drum, another a flute, and a third man danced out of the shadows. He wore a raven mask and had long, weedy hair that wriggled like snakes about his body. He danced round her, brushing her with a skinny, crooked root that had raven feathers pushed into one end.

Her feet started moving on their own; then she was dancing round and round him, the drum like the beat of her heart.

The dancing man brushed and brushed at her, and as the feathers slid along her skin, her mouth and her nose grew stiff and stretched until they were a raven's beak, her burned arm straightened, both arms grew shiny black feathers until they were wings not arms, and she was dancing half on air, half on the ground.

The building faded.

She was flying high above the mountains.

The air changed; it was warmer, and it smelled different. She looked down and saw her house.

It was all lit up, a police car out front, red lights flashing.

She glided down, landed in the backyard, and was herself again the moment her feet touched ground, same old Mercy with the scarred face and crooked arm. And in big trouble. She smoothed her hand down the front of the ripped and bloody dress. *If I can just get up to my room and change, maybe it won't be so bad.*

The kitchen door opened, and her father came out. He was looking back, talking to someone still in the house. "She likes to fool around in the woods over . . . Mercy!" He caught her by the shoulders and started shaking her and shouting at her. "How many times . . . how many times have I told you . . . what happened to you? Who did this . . . what . . . ?"

She broke free with a strength she didn't know she had, at first angry because he was angry. Then his skin peeled away and she saw his naked, bloody heart and she read what was written there, not revulsion, but love mixed with a terrible guilt because he hadn't been with them when the steering went on the car, because he hadn't been there to pull her from the fire, because he'd put off having the car serviced. Each time he looked at her, he remembered he hadn't been there, remembered all the things he hadn't done.

With a gasp, she flung herself at her father, hugged him hard. "Don't worry about me, Da. You don't need to worry about me ever." She hugged him again, looked up at him, smiling, knowing what she had to say. "It was just this silly porcupine, Da. He got caught and I had to get him loose, but he didn't like it much and he kept struggling. Sorta like me sometimes, huh?"

It was a lie and she didn't feel comfortable about that, but her father relaxed, his worst fears wiped away. He smiled back at her, shaking his head. "You and animals, Mercy, I don't know what I'm going to do with you."

She leaned against him and let him take her into the house. He didn't realize it yet, but lots of things were going to be changing. She wasn't angry anymore; she wasn't afraid. And she wasn't going to let her father use her to pay imaginary debts.

Same old Mercy. But never the same again.

Kushtakas *are folk who have a transforming encounter with a land otter, becoming otters themselves with some human features left. They have the power of illusion, can be invisible or appear as a sister, a mother, a father, a brother. They kidnap children, possess bodies, cause storms and famine, yet they can also be benevolent, saving those lost at sea or in the woods and granting power to any shaman strong enough to wrest it from them.*

Tales of the Sidhi-kur

~~~~~~

Pamela F. Service

The wind blew from the distant stars. Cold and wild, it blew across the Mongolian steppe, singing its winter song of endless cold, cold deeper than the grave.

Through the walls of the yurt, Batu listened and shivered. Pulling his sheepskin jacket more tightly around him, he shuffled closer to where the fire glowed in the center of his family's snug, round home. Across from him, amid a nest of blankets, his mother was feeding the baby. By the yellow light of an oil lamp, his father was fixing a broken leather bridle.

They had eaten dinner already, but tonight there was no singing or storytelling. The night seemed too wild and cold to push back merely with words. On such nights surely spirits rode the wind, and one would not want to attract their attention.

So Batu just squatted by the fire and looked into its glowing coals.

Tonight, even their yurt's thick felt and latticework walls were sliced through by the cold. His face tingled as if pricked by needles, and the metal fittings on the door were furred with frost. Half sleeping, Batu listened to the cold, wordless song of the wind.

Then he seemed to hear words in that song. A voice, a human voice. Batu raised his head. His father dropped the bridle, and his mother turned from the baby. Rising and going to the door, his father lifted the latch and pushed open the wooden door against the wind. "Hello!" he called into the raging night. "Who is there?"

"It is I," a voice came back on the wind. "A wandering traveler who has lost his way. I pray you give me shelter."

"Indeed and gladly," Batu's father called back. "No living thing should be abroad on such a night."

A dark shape filled the doorway; then a man stooped and entered. He was tall and thin. His coat, hat, and boots were of dark fur, but his face was pale with the cold. Frost whitened his beard and mustache, and his eyes glinted in the firelight like black jewels.

"Welcome, honored sir," Batu's parents both said, anxious to play host in a land where visitors were few. "We have only just finished dining, and the mutton stew is still warm. Will you honor us by eating some?"

Sitting on a rug by the fire, the man nodded. "Indeed it has been a long while since I have eaten."

Batu's mother served the stranger a big bowl of stew and a smaller bowl of tea strengthened with yak butter. Smiling and nodding, he finished everything and a second and third helping as well. Finally he set aside his bowls and sat back comfortably.

"Come now," the stranger said, "it is a wild, uncanny night. Let us drive back the dark by telling stories."

Now, with this stranger in the yurt, the night seemed less

threatening. Storytelling would be welcome, Batu thought, and smiled to see his father agreeing.

"A story indeed! Shall I begin or you?"

"Ah," the stranger said. "I am known for my storytelling. Let me begin and pay for my supper. What say we have a tale of the Sidhi-kur?"

At this, Batu let out a laugh, then, hand to mouth, he politely tried to hide it.

His father frowned at him and quickly said to the stranger, "Take no offense. It is just that the boy hears many tales of the Sidhi-kur, because those are ones I know."

The stranger's eyes glinted. "Ah, but there are as many tales of the Sidhi-kur as there are stars in the winter sky. Perhaps I will tell one you do not know."

The man's smile emboldened Batu to say, "Any story you tell will be very welcome, honored sir. But also I laughed because whenever father tells a Sidhi-kur story, we argue. I say the prince is a great fool, and my father says I am a great fool to think so."

The stranger nodded, smiling a thin, pale smile. "Let me then begin with the beginning that we all know and go on to a tale within the tale. Perhaps then we shall see where wisdom lies."

He sat back, the fire casting shadows over his bony face as his voice slid into the deep rhythms of a tale teller.

~

Once there was a prince who wished to learn the secrets of magic, so he traveled to the cave of a master magician. But there he accidentally angered the master, and he offered to do any task the master set him that he might gain the magician's forgiveness and his blessing.

So the master magician said, "There is a magical living corpse, the Sidhi-kur, who will bring endless gold and long life to any who control him. I would have you fetch this dead thing and bring him here to me."

"I will," said the prince. "Tell me what I must do."

"Walk one league from here, and you will come to a dark, wooded ravine, fearfully deep and cold. It is strewn with the graves of giants, and they will rise up and come at you. But if you chant the magic words 'hala svaha' and scatter an offering of this enchanted barley, they will fall back and let you pass.

"A league farther on, you will come to a broad cold-water meadow in which are the graves of smaller men. They, too, will rise up and not let you pass unless you chant the words 'hulu svaha' and scatter an offering of enchanted barley.

"Finally, a league farther on, you will find a garden beautiful with flowers and cool with fountains. There the corpses of children will rise from the earth and bar your way unless you scatter barley and chant the words 'rira phat.'

"Beyond there is the cold, dark forest wherein dwells the master of the magic dead, the Sidhi-kur. His body glows like pale silver beneath his robes, and on seeing you he will flee to the top of his sacred tree from which he gains his strength. Go there taking this great white ax and threaten to chop down his tree if he does not come down and give himself over to you. To save his tree, he will do so, and you must place him in this many-colored sack. He is light as bones, and you can easily carry him to me on your back.

"But mark me," the magician said, looking forcefully at the prince. "Once you set out on the return trip, you must not say a single thing, not one word must pass your lips, until you arrive here."

So taking the enchanted barley, the white ax, and the many-colored sack, the prince set out. All happened as the magician had foretold. Scattering the enchanted barley and saying the magic words, he safely passed through each group of risen dead until at last he came to the Sidhi-kur. In a flash of silver, the living corpse fled through the cold forest to the top of his sacred tree, but to spare it from the prince's ax he agreed to descend and allow himself to be carried off in the many-colored sack.

Once they were on the road, the Sidhi-kur said from within the sack, "Since the way ahead is long and the journey tedious, let us pass the time by telling stories."

But remembering the magician's warning, the prince said not a word.

"Well then," said the Sidhi-kur, "if you will not tell a story, I will tell one. This is the tale of the Rival Artists."

~

Once there was a khan, a ruler, who delighted in building fine palaces and temples. He gathered to himself all the finest builders and artists, and they vied with each other to see who could do the best work and most please the khan. Chief among these rivals were an excellent woodcarver and a splendid painter. They carved and painted the fine decorations that finished each of the new buildings, and the khan could not decide which of them was the greatest artist.

At last the old khan died, and his son became khan in his place. The painter saw in this a chance to rid himself of his great rival.

He stayed away from the court for several days and then appeared before the khan, saying, "Oh Great Khan, your father has been born again in the Land of the Gods. As I was always his favorite artist, he sent for me that I might return here and deliver to you this letter."

The painter then handed the young khan a letter that he, knowing the old khan's writing, had forged.

The letter said: "My beloved son, being reborn in the Land of the Gods, I am greatly content for I have been building here a fine temple, far greater than any before. It now lacks only the fine carving that my master carver alone can do. I bid you send him here that I may complete this great work."

The khan, wishing to please his father, sent for the wood-carver, then asked the painter how a living man might be sent to the Land of the Gods.

"Your father instructed that the carver should gather all his tools and stand in an open place surrounded by piles of wood soaked with sesame oil. These shall be set afire, and as your musicians play loud and sacred music, a great steed of smoke shall rise up and carry the woodcarver to the Land of the Gods."

The woodcarver suspected that this was a plot by his rival, but not daring to defy the khan's order he agreed to go in seven days' time once he had assembled all the tools and wood he needed.

Then he returned home and by day gathered the wood in a field near his house. But by night he and his wife dug a tunnel between his house and the center of the circle of wood.

When the seventh day came, the khan and his court assembled in the field. The woodcarver took his tools and stood in the center of the oiled wood, and it was set afire. As the smoke billowed up, the painter pointed, saying, "See, there goes the sacred smoke steed carrying the woodcarver to the Land of the Gods." The others, not admitting they could see no such sacred steed, agreed.

But while the musicians played loud enough to hide any screaming, the woodcarver, hidden by the smoke, stepped into the secret tunnel and crawled safely to his home. There he remained for one month, keeping out of the tanning sunlight and bathing himself every day in milk until he was very pale.

Then, dressing in a fine new robe, he walked to the court of the khan and said, "Oh Great Khan, I have returned from the Land of the Gods and bring you this letter from your father."

He then handed over a letter that he, also knowing the old khan's writing, had forged. It read: "Beloved son, due to the fine artistry of our woodcarver, my temple is more splendid than ever. I bid you shower on this woodcarver all honor and wealth as reward. My temple now lacks but the fine painting that only our great painter can do. I bid you send him now to me in the same manner as you sent the woodcarver and on his return reward him in the same way."

On hearing this, the painter was astonished. He had thought his rival dead, yet here he stood radiant and alive and being showered with wealth and honor. Perhaps he had indeed traveled to the Land of the Gods, the painter thought, and if he himself were not to be outstripped by the carver, he must do the same.

On the appointed day, the painter stood with his tools in an open field. The oiled wood was set ablaze, and as the music played loud enough to hide any screaming, the woodcarver pointed to the rising clouds of smoke and said, "There, see the painter going to his just reward."

Then he returned home with this wife to enjoy many years of fame and wealth.

~

As the Sidhi-kur finished this tale from within the many-colored sack, the prince exclaimed, "Aha! That woodcarver was not only a great artist but a wise one!"

The prince thus forgot the magician's warning not to speak while on the journey. When these words were uttered, the Sidhi-kur burst from the sack and in a flash of silver flew back to his forest, calling out, "Wisdom is not for everyone!"

~

"You see, you see!" Batu burst out as the stranger finished his story. "No one could be as foolish as that prince. There are hundreds of Sidhi-kur stories, and at the end of each one the prince forgets the magician's warning and says something.

43

Then, flash, the Sidhi-kur flies off, and the prince has to start all over. How could anyone forget what was really happening again and again?"

His parents started apologizing for their son's rudeness, but the pale stranger shook his head and smiled at Batu. "So, you doubt that words have magic? You doubt that a story has the power to make itself seem real?"

"Not enough to fool a wise prince."

"Oh, and you are a wise boy, then?" The stranger laughed. "Let us see. You make the same bargain as the prince. I will tell other stories of the Sidhi-kur, and you must remain silent until our evening of storytelling is over."

Batu's parents chuckled to see how their troublesome son had been tricked into not interrupting. But Batu only nodded. Grinning broadly, he said nothing.

The fire glinting darkly in his eyes, the stranger began another tale.

~

So the prince, seeing that he had lost the object of his quest, turned around and walked back through the three places of the dead, enchanting them as he had before until he came to the cold forest where the Sidhi-kur, in a flash of silver, fled before him to the top of his tree. But when the prince made as if to chop down the tree, the Sidhi-kur agreed to climb down and go again into the many-colored sack.

After they had been traveling for a while, the Sidhi-kur said from the depth of the sack, "The way ahead is long and the journey tedious. Let us pass the time by telling stories." But the prince marched silently ahead.

"Very well. If you will not tell a story, I will," said the Sidhi-kur. "This is the tale of the three brothers."

~

There once were three brothers. The eldest was a mighty warrior who exulted in battle. The youngest brother was a skilled hunter who thrilled at tracking wild beasts. The third was a quiet herdsman who was content to follow his herds across the open steppe.

The three saw little of each other except during the summer gathering of their people. At one such meeting, the three strolled together talking beside a stream in a valley. Stopping, they stared at an island within the stream where sat a beautiful young maiden. She was so lovely and gentle seeming as she sat there braiding flowers, that each brother resolved to make her his wife.

At that moment the stream boiled and out plunged a hideous demon astride a black water horse. Reaching down, the demon grabbed the frightened girl and rode off with her out of the valley.

The three brothers ran for their horses, mounted, and rode after the demon, each one hoping to save the girl and make her his own. All day they rode, the figure of the demon a distant dot far ahead of them. Toward evening, they came to a mountain pass where travelers had piled up offering stones into a cairn. The eldest and youngest brothers wanted to press on, but the middle brother said that they must stop and make a stone offering to the mountain spirits.

As they did so, an old man stepped from a rocky cleft and asked where they were riding in such haste. When they answered that they chased a demon who had stolen a beautiful girl, he beckoned them toward his cleft.

"We waste time!" the eldest brother exclaimed. "I would make that girl my wife by using my skill with the sword."

"We must ride on," said the youngest brother, "but it is my skill with the bow that will win her."

Yet the middle brother said, "Surely this old hermit is a holy man and perhaps can help us in our quest." So saying, he dismounted and walked to the cleft, his brothers following.

The hermit pointed to the back of the crevasse. "Behold, three things with which one might overcome the perils of the road ahead. Choose wisely, and one of you may win what you seek."

With a triumphant cry, the eldest brother ran forward and seized a great jeweled sword. Likewise the youngest brother hurried to claim a golden bow and arrows set with peacock feathers. More slowly the middle brother walked toward his choice: a thin, mangy-looking, yellow dog. The dog smelled his offered hand and wagged its tail.

When the brothers returned to their horses, the hermit had gone. They mounted and continued on the trail, though the demon was now out of sight.

The weapons of the eldest and youngest brothers gleamed proudly in the setting sun, but the yellow dog whined and could not keep up, so the middle brother stopped and carried it on his horse. When he did, he was astonished to hear the dog say the word "Mangalam." He spoke kindly to the dog, and ever and anon the dog repeated the same word, "Mangalam."

As the sun set, the moon rose, showing them plainly the trail. At last it led them to a thorny valley where the moon shone on a great scattering of bones, horns, and antlers.

"There has been a great hunt here!" exclaimed the youngest brother. "See all the game that was slaughtered. I am sorry to have missed it."

At the voice of the hunter, the bones, hooves, and antlers began to stir. Night wind blew among them with the sound of snuffling and growls. The bones rose up and came together,

46

moonlight clothing them with the misty shapes of dead beasts. Eyes gleamed, and teeth and hooves glinted like knives as the phantoms glided toward the brothers.

"This is for me!" the youngest brother yelled, and taking his bow and arrows, he began shooting into the ghostly pack. At once, the ghosts came at him like a great wind. In moments, teeth and claws, horns and hooves tore apart the youngest brother and his mount. Then vengeful eyes turned on the remaining brothers.

The eldest brother drew his sword, but the middle brother clutched his frightened dog and called out, "Mangalam!"

At once the ghostly beasts vanished into mist, and their bones clattered lifeless to the ground.

Grieving to leave their brother's bones scattered with the rest, the two brothers rode out of the thorny valley until they came to a desolate plain. All about them, the moonlight gleamed off helmets and armor encasing dry, white bones.

"There has been a great battle here!" exclaimed the eldest brother. "See all the warriors that were killed. I am sorry to have missed it."

At the voice of the warrior, the armored bones began to stir. Night wind blew among them with the whisper of angry voices. Clattering, the armor and bones came together, and mist clung about them in the form of dead warriors. Eyes glowed like coals, and swords glimmered with moonlight as the phantom army rushed toward the brothers.

"This is for me!" the eldest brother yelled, and he drove his horse into the ghostly horde, swinging his jeweled sword to the right and left. Like lightning in a great storm, the swords of the dead flashed and soon hacked apart the eldest brother and his mount. Then fierce eyes turned on the remaining brother.

Clutching his trembling dog, the middle brother yelled out, "Mangalam!" and at once the ghostly warriors crumpled to the ground, their bones and battered armor lying as lifeless as before.

Grieving to leave his brother's bones scattered with the rest, the middle brother rode swiftly from the desolate plain until he came to a rocky outcrop about which lay bowls and dishes with the dried remains of offerings.

"There must have been a great ceremony here," said the middle brother. "See all the offerings lying about. I am sorry to have missed it."

At the herdsman's voice, the rocky outcrop seemed to stir in the moonlight. Night wind blew about it with the sound of hissing and chittering, and dark shapes peeled from its surface. With eyes cold as gleaming ice, rock spirits floated like shadows toward the middle brother.

"I have no offerings for you, spirits!" he cried, clutching the shivering dog. "Do not harm us. Mangalam!"

At once the hungry spirits swept back to their rocks, and quickly the herdsman brother rode away from the shadowy outcrop.

At last before him lay a moon-glimmering pool, and on an island in its center sat the lovely maiden. On seeing the herdsman, she rose and stretched out her arms to him. "You have come to rescue me from the demon. To do so, you have only to kill the yellow dog you have brought with you, and I am yours." The girl threw over to him a golden knife with which to kill the dog.

Holding the dog, the herdsman dismounted from his horse and called, "No, that I cannot do. This dog has been loyal to me and taught me the word of power, the blessing Mangalam."

At the sound of that word, the golden knife flew back across the pool and plunged into the maiden's heart. She screamed, and her body turned into that of the demon. The creature burst into flame, writhing and screaming until the smoke of its burning blew away on the wind.

48

Astonished, the herdsman saw that he now held in his arms not the yellow dog but the lovely maiden returned to her true form. Together they mounted his horse and rode happily across the steppe to his distant yurt.

As the Sidhi-kur finished his tale from within the many-colored sack, the prince exclaimed, "Truly wise words have greater power than any weapons!"

When the prince, thus forgetting the magician's warning, uttered these words, the Sidhi-kur burst from the sack. In a flash of silver, the living corpse flew back to his cold forest, calling out, "Wisdom is not for everyone!"

"There! You see?" Batu cried. "No one could be as foolish as that prince! He again forgot the warning."

The stranger burst into laughter. "And so, foolish boy, have you. Under the enchantment of words, you forgot our agreement!"

With that, a flash of silver filled the yurt, and the stranger was gone. Only his words hung in the cold air. "Indeed, wisdom is not for everyone!"

Batu's parents' eyes were wide and their faces pale, but they said not a word. Quickly they prepared for bed—banking the fire, closing the smoke flap, and blowing out the lamp.

Lying in the dark, wrapped in his blankets, Batu listened for a long while to the cold winter wind blowing beyond the walls.

The years would pass and he would gain much wisdom, but never again could Batu listen to the wind without hearing in it laughter cold as death.

Pamela F. Service

In Mongolian folklore, the Sidhi-kur is a being of strange magical abilities, a living corpse who has power over the dead and who gains strength from his sacred tree. He may give aid to anyone who is clever enough to outwit him.

Enter the Night

~~~~~~

Laura Resnick

Young, I was so very young the night the Ixtabay called to me. The years have passed, my eyes have dimmed, my once-smooth face now bears a white and bristly beard, and the laughter of my grandchildren echoes faintly in the hollow well of my ears. But once I was young and heard her call.

The rains have come and gone many, many times since that mad moment I entered the night of the Ixtabay, but when the village is silent in sleep, when the hungry growl of the jungle cools to a soft murmur of satiation, when my heart is open to the spirit voices that rule the night—then do I hear her again, calling to me across the void of the tens of thousands of nights that I have endured without her.

~

Deep in the jungle, so deep that even today no paved road reaches it, our village perched on the banks of the river. My grandfather's tiny,

51

unpainted house sat so close to the water that it looked as though it might fling itself into the current at any moment. My mother and I lived in it with him. I remembered little of my father, who died when I was very small.

"He disappeared into the jungle one night. You see, the Ixtabay called to him," Grandfather would say to me when my mother was not listening. "And, not heeding my warnings, he went to her." Then Grandfather would sigh and shake his head.

Once or twice, though, my mother heard him, and then her dark eyes sparked with anger as she scolded him. "You must not flood the boy's ears with such superstitious nonsense," she would snap. "His father got lost in the jungle and crawled home half-alive, then died of fever three days later."

Grandfather would sigh and shrug and roll his eyes at me. As soon as her attention was diverted, he would whisper, "He followed the Ixtabay into the bush and, like all her lovers, went insane."

I didn't really know what the Ixtabay was, and it was several more years before I had even the slightest idea what a lover was. But I would listen respectfully to the old man, just as I listened respectfully to my mother when she told me to ignore his strange stories and warnings.

I had no fear of the jungle by day. I hunted and fished to help provide for our table, and when my work was done, I played with the other boys like a wild animal. The ruins of an ancient Mayan city lay buried in the forest, its crumbling walls covered by vines, its tumbled temple shaded by palm trees and swamp cypresses. We scrambled across the damp, mysterious stones, heedless of tales of ghosts, demons, and the vengeful spirits of the unbaptized dead. The British and American archaeologists who scour Central America for such ruins did not yet know of this place, nor did anyone from our village ever consider telling them. The dead should be left in peace, my grandfather said, and the jungle should be allowed to devour her prey.

Yes, the jungle by day was a place of infinite wonders and pleasures. Emerald green and scarlet red birds flew overhead as we capered and crawled through the jungle's fragrant undergrowth. Sapote trees were abundant, with their salmon-pink fruit which makes such a sweet snack, though I preferred the yellow, jellylike flesh found inside the leathery seedpods of the scarcer guava tree. Orange, lime, avocado, mango, and papaya tumbled out of the green canopy over our heads, nourishing us as we chased lizards, swam naked in the streams, hid from adults amid the tough trunks of the banana trees, and explored the ruined city of the ancient ones. In all the world, there was no better place than the jungle by day.

But at night, the jungle changed and became a place of unseen dangers and oft-told horrors. Shrill screeches and strange cries came from its depths. The friendly paths we had made by day disappeared at night as mist, shadow, and darkness obscured everything and trees reached out to embrace the unwary walker in their deadly grasp. In those days, so long ago, a small child was still carried away every so often by a night-hunting puma, and even the beautiful ocelot and tiny margay appeared ferocious after nightfall. The tasty iguana seemed like a dragon in the dark, and the little white bats became the vampires of my nightmares as they flapped and flashed into the opaque belly of the night. The evil yellow jaw—Tommygoff came out from beneath its rocks and low bushes to hunt in the dark, swinging and jumping from trees or slithering along the ground, legless and silent. More than eight feet long, it was aggressive and would usually strike more than once. I used to believe that such a creature must have killed my father, but my mother told me that its poison kills a man much more quickly than my father died.

No earthly creature, however, was as terrifying as the spirit creatures that rose through the mist after the sun had set. They conquered the manless jungle by night and made it their own, and I knew that it was their voices I heard shrieking and growling on the heavy tropical air as I lay in my cot and prayed to the Virgin and all the gods.

There was, of course, the Greasy Man, who haunted the forsaken ruined city near our village. Closer to home, there was the Ashi de Pompi, who hid in the abandoned hovels of burned-out dwellings. If children were too noisy, these monsters stirred at night and punished them with horrible vengeance.

A far more dreadful beast, however, was the Sisimito, a huge, hairy creature that kidnapped small children in the hope of learning how to talk. The Sisimito loved fire but did not know how to make it, so he left piles of kindling everywhere, believing that one might start spontaneously. If drawn to a man's fire, the Sisimito would stare at it until the embers grew cold, then eat them. Besides children, the Sisimito loved captured women and would steal maidens and young wives who ventured away from home after dark. Luckily, my grandfather taught me how to escape from the Sisimito.

"His feet point backward," the old man explained to me. "So when you see him, just hide behind a bush very quickly. Confused, he will look around for you. When he sees his own footprints, he'll think they're yours and follow them, going back the way he came."

A healthy boy with a well-developed sense of self-preservation, I feared all these creatures. But there was nothing I feared as much as the duendes. They were dwarves with flat, yellow faces, long arms, thick legs, and heavy shoulders, and their bodies were covered with short brown hair. Duendes had only four fingers and were jealous of anyone who had five, so my grandfather taught me to salute them with my thumb concealed in the palm of my hand.

Among their hideous deeds, Duendes were said to carry away dogs. I knew it was true, for in my twelfth year, my beloved pet Dog-Dog disappeared for a whole night. He crawled out of the jungle at dawn, barely alive and missing one leg. I knew the Duendes had torn it off when I searched the jungle south of the village and found their pointed-heel footprints mingled with his blood.

The ancient ones knew about these creatures, too, carving their images into the stone walls of their temples and palaces. One day my three-legged dog and I uncovered strange carvings in the ruined city, and Dog-Dog barked wildly at the portraits of naked, four-fingered, pointed-heeled dwarves grinning maliciously and wearing banana fronds on their heads.

But by my seventeenth year, not even the fear of Duendes could keep me from answering the call of the Ixtabay.

~

There was a girl named Chikki in the village downriver from us. I had never seen such a girl, and my soul was consumed with wonder. No girl in the world had hair so black, lashes so long, teeth so white, skin so golden. She beckoned to me with a shy, promising smile that spoke of mysteries so fantastic they blurred my vision, made my hands clumsy, and numbed my ears to my mother's questions and my grandfather's warnings.

Her family did not approve of me—a fatherless boy from upriver, with a crazy grandfather, a three-legged dog, and no prospects to speak of—and forbade Chikki to see me. So we met secretly amid the whispering stones of the Mayan ruins, hiding in the shadows and listening for the approach of the boys who played like wild animals. But the touch of her hand on mine, the glow in her eyes, the honeyed sound of her voice dulled my senses to all else, including the sound of footsteps; and so her eldest brother caught us one day.

Chikki's movements were watched so closely after that day that it was impossible for us to meet again. Happily, her younger sister found our predicament wildly romantic and offered to carry messages between us. Our words were brief and to the point. We would run off and get married, and then no one could keep us apart ever again. We agreed to meet after nightfall in the jungle, where there was no chance of anyone seeing us. I chose a spot very near her village so she wouldn't have to go far alone; though many young men my age had long since ceased believing in the orphans of the night, I remembered the pointed-heel footprints I had once found mingled with the blood of my three-legged dog, and I knew the tropical night guarded the secrets of another realm. I was ready to risk everything for Chikki, but I would not let her risk her safety in the lush, shrieking darkness.

I carried a torch the night I went to meet Chikki, a flaming lantern to frighten away night-hunting cats, the yellow jaw—Tommygoff, and the feisty peccary. I kept to the path, which, to my relief, did not disappear after dark. Without the torch, though, I'd have lost it in minutes and stumbled blindly into the reaching arms of the rustling trees, thick with vines and heavy with the scent of orchids. For the first time ever, I wondered why my father had not taken a torch with him the night he had wandered away from our village and into the forest; didn't he know he would surely get lost without one?

Ignoring the gibbering, growling, and chattering of the night, I summoned the courage of young manhood and plunged into the heart of darkness, impelled ever forward by love, excitement, and, yes, a young man's desire for his bride. The strength of my passion must have shielded me, I thought, for no Sisimito came forth to admire my flaming torch, and the bloodthirsty yellow-faced, four-fingered Duendes stayed hidden in their lairs. Even the normal, earthy sounds of the jungle faded away as I recklessly thrust through the bush, until the night was still and only the sound of my breathing remained. And that was when I heard her song for the first time.

It was a song without words, a lullaby without beginning or end. It entered my mind slowly, stealing across my senses as twilight steals across the sky, until I realized that I had been listening to it for some time. It was a woman's voice, soft, sweet, and warm. But what woman would be in the jungle at night? Only one that I could think of.

"Chikki?" I called. She must have grown impatient waiting for me, or perhaps she was afraid of being seen at our meeting place. "Chikki? Is that you?"

The song grew stronger, as if she were calling to me. She was much nearer now. Off the path, somewhere in the dense foliage to my right. "Chikki?"

A woman's laughter. Light, happy, alluring. My heart started to pound. "Chikki? Where are you?" More laughter, beckoning me. "Chikki, come out of there. You'll get lost."

The song, sweet with promise, drew me to the edge of the path and invited me into the wild unknown. Her voice rose and fell smoothly, lilting and entrancing. I had no thought of resisting as I stepped off the well-worn path and entered the night.

The jungle reached out for me, its branches enfolding me, its vines reaching up to embrace my legs. I stumbled and strayed, but the song always guided me back to her, until I could feel her all around me.

"Where are you?" I cried at last, still not seeing her.

There was laughter over my head. I looked up into the branches of a vast, leafy sapote tree. There sat the Ixtabay, combing her hair. And such hair it was! Blacker than night, it rippled like water and shone like polished obsidian. It was so long that she could sit on it, and it caught the flickering light of my torch and glittered like the night sky embedded with stars.

In her pale hand, she held a jewel-encrusted comb—a gift from some long-ago Spanish prince?—which she drew through the shining waves of her hair again and again in a rhythm as hypnotic as that of her song. Her skin was as pearl-white as the inside of a perfect coconut; her body was soft and shapely and graceful beyond any dream of womanhood. I gazed at her in mute adoration and fell hopelessly, helplessly in love. And the fiery gleam in her amber eyes told me she knew it.

"Beware the Ixtabay," my grandfather had said so many times in my childhood. "Beware that dainty demon!"

But he could not have known, I thought, staring thunderstruck at her loveliness. *How could he have possibly known?* There could be no evil, no danger in such perfect beauty.

"She hypnotizes onlookers, who follow her into the bush and go insane," Grandfather always said, and I wondered why my father had been so foolhardy.

But now I knew, yes, now I understood why my father had followed her. There could be no other choice. The warm promise of her smile, the graceful poetry of her gestures, the lilting sigh of her song, and the mysterious glow in her eyes all offered a gift greater and more powerful than any lingering fear of danger.

As in legend, she descended from her tree and walked above the surface of the ground, each small, pale foot stepping lightly on the misty air as she led me deeper into the bush. So entranced was I that I let my torch drop from my hand. It fell upon the damp earth, sizzled, and died. I hesitated for only a moment, then I saw the gleaming curve of her arm in the dim moonlight as she beckoned me to follow, and I could no more resist her lure than I could will myself to stop breathing.

～

They found me in the jungle, feverish, raving, and unable to account for the three days I had been missing. Upon hearing the news, Chikki became convinced that I would die without her. She defied her family and came to our village, moving into my grandfather's house to help my mother nurse me. I would have died even so, but my grandfather—against my mother's wishes—brought an obeah-man to the village to brew potions, chant spells, and fight against the curse that had come upon me. The man placed gourds filled with food in the doorway to ward off sickness brought by duendes, crossed my worn shoes in order to prevent evil spirits from entering them during my sleep, painted the indigo cross on my forehead, fed me broth made from the flesh of the wowla, and chased the fatal magic of the Ixtabay out of my soul. But though I lived, he could never chase her from my heart.

I heard the faint stirring of her song for many long, tormented nights, and I often broke my promise to resist it. Usually someone would stop me before I could escape from our tiny house, and more than once they resorted to tying me to the bed. But once I tricked them all into thinking I was too weak to warrant a guard, and I slipped into the dark jungle before anyone could catch me. They chased me all night, their torches a banner of man in that otherwise manless world as I crashed blindly through branches, fronds, and twining vines, searching for the love that, having welcomed me but once, would now elude me forever.

They brought me home at dawn, shaking and demented, wishing for the same peace that had ended my father's torment so long ago. How could I go on living if I was never again to know the embrace of the Ixtabay? All other pleasures in life tasted bitter after such sweetness.

In time, the hated obeah-man succeeded in dimming the Ixta-bay's teasing, haunting voice, until her song was only a hollow echo in my memory. Pronounced fit in mind and body, I married Chikki and built a small house for her, well away from the forest's edge. We had children who, like the seasons, ripened and eventually bore fruit of their own. And had I never heard the voice of the Ixtabay, I would say that mine had been a happy life.

Now I am old, and my daughter tells my grandchildren to ignore my strange stories and warnings.

"You must stop filling their ears with such nonsense," she snaps at me. "Duendes, three-legged dogs, the Ashi de Pompi, and the Sisimito. Hah! These are modern times. No one believes that foolishness anymore."

Yes, these are modern times, but once in a while, a dog disappears without a trace, except for the strange footprints that mingle with his in the damp earth. And every so often, a young man returns from the jungle with a haunted soul that makes him rave until death claims him. Modern times disappear when night descends upon the forest.

And so I tell my grandsons, "Beware the Ixtabay, beware that dainty demon!" I want them to know more peace than I have known during the tens of thousands of nights that I have endured without her.

Chikki has joined the ancestors now, and I am alone when darkness falls. Now, when the village is silent in sleep, when the hungry growl of the jungle cools to a soft murmur of satiation, when my heart is open to the spirit voices that rule the night— then do I hear the Ixtabay again, calling to me across the void of years. And I know that soon, at last, I will enter the night once more and join her forever in that other realm.

Belize is a small country in Central America, on the Gulf Coast. Though it is no larger than Massachusetts, its topography is quite varied, comprising rain forests, jungles, mountains, coast plains, and islands. Many different cultures converge in this little corner of the world, including Mayan, Hispanic, British, and African. Their legends have peopled the mysterious forests and jungles with many strange, unearthly creatures, such as the Ixtabay, *said to be the vengeful spirit of a woman who died for love and who now seeks to lure men to their deaths.*

Fitting In

~~~~~~

Lawrence Schimel

The Doppelgänger
is like the perpetual kid brother:
always hanging around the edges
trying to be just like you.

You and your friends pretend not to
  notice him,
as if he just doesn't exist.

And that's when the Doppelgänger
  strikes.
When everyone's busy
looking the other way.

He makes you disappear.
And he puts on your clothes,
your blue-and-white T-shirt with the
  pizza stain,
your favorite sneakers,
even your baseball cap, which he
  puts on backward
just like you always do.

He knows how to be you better
  than you ever did.
He's studied you carefully,

every minor detail, every peculiar habit,
and now he's so much like you
that no one even knows you're gone.
He uses the same curses you like to use,
he walks just like you,
and he takes over your life.
And at last he fits in.
Until he gets bored
and moves on to some other kid.

This could never happen to you, you think.
You'd notice him hanging around
and do something to stop him.

But what if he was already somebody else?
What if one of your friends
hadn't been smart enough,
observant enough,
and one day, when no one was looking
and your friend was feeling like he just didn't fit in,
he got disappeared?

Suddenly, you look more carefully at everyone around you,
checking for any sudden changes
in their behavior,
waiting for that moment when the Doppelgänger forgets
who he is, and says something
your friend would never say,
something the *last* kid the Doppelgänger took over
used to say.

"You're crazy, man," your best friend tells you
and you laugh, pretending it was all a joke,
and forget all about Doppelgängers.

Until now.

Now, when your kid brother's been acting kind of funny
and you can't help but wonder . . .
If, one day, while you weren't looking . . .
Nah, it couldn't be.

But . . .
But what if your brother really *is* a Doppelgänger?

And he wants you next!

*The Doppelgänger is exactly what the name says it is—if you
know German. It translates roughly as "double goer." The Doppelgänger is a creature who can change the shape of its body
until it looks like any person, male or female. Once it looks like
you, it kills you, eats your body, then pretends to be you.*

The Bleeding Moon

~~~~~~

Harry Turtledove

P etko, Todor, and Georgi were three cousins who lived in the village of Gramada. The Turks had overrun Gramada—along with the rest of Bulgaria—a century and a half before but hardly seemed to know they had. It was only a small village, after all, off in the woods in the far northwest. Once a year Symeon, the headman, would take some sheep to the Turkish beg in Vidin, down by the Danube. That kept the official happy, and he left Gramada alone.

One morning, the cousins decided to go hunting. They gathered in front of Petko's house with bows and spears and cudgels. In the village, only Symeon and his brother, Rossen, owned muskets. "We'll bring back rabbits for a stew," Petko called to his mother, Zhivka, "or maybe partridges or pheasant."

"Or a fat deer," Todor said, "or even a boar." He was eighteen, a couple of years older than the other two cousins. His beard was beginning to sprout thickly on his cheeks and chin and upper lip. Petko envied him for that. But because Todor was so close to being a man, he sometimes thought he knew more than he did and could do more than he could. Petko didn't envy him there, for he got himself into trouble he could have avoided.

Zhivka had seen that, too. She wagged her forefinger at all three youths. "You stick together," she said sternly. "I don't want any of you running into the men from Kula by himself." A few weeks before, a girl from Kula had run off to marry a boy from Gramada without her parents' leave, and there was bad blood between the villages. Feuds had started for less.

"All right, Mother," Petko said. Georgi nodded, too. He was within a month or two of Petko's age, a little shorter, a little stockier, his brown hair a shade lighter. Anyone could tell at a glance that they were related.

Todor nodded, too, a moment later than he should have. Zhivka raised her dark eyebrows. Petko didn't blame her. He wouldn't have trusted that nod, either. But then Todor said, "Let's go!" And off they went. Petko looked back over his shoulder. His mother stood watching them for a little while, then walked over to the garden to weed the turnip patch.

Petko glanced over at Todor. "If we see a boar, the best thing for us to do is get up a tree fast as we can, before it rips us to pieces."

"Ah, you're still milk-fed, that's what's wrong with you. Me, I like a nice piece of meat, with the hot fat burning my mouth when I bite into it." Todor smacked his lips.

"Call me milk-fed again, and you'll be sorry," Petko said. He hoped that wouldn't start a brawl: His cousin was bigger and stronger and meaner, too. But if you let somebody push you around once, he'd think he could do it all the time.

Todor didn't go on with it, not today. The three cousins walked along a dirt track through the fields where wheat and barley grew. Petko's father, Vulko, straightened up from weeding, saw them, and waved. They all waved back.

Gramada and the fields and meadows around it were like a little island in a big sea of forest. The woods were a different world. Petko loved and dreaded them at the same time. All sorts of treasures came from the forest: game and timber and honey and mushrooms and herbs. But you couldn't afford to forget danger lurked there, too: bears and wolves and other, darker things.

And now, as Petko's mother had said, the men of Kula were liable to be up in arms because of that girl. Petko wished he and his cousins weren't heading northwest; Kula lay in that direction. But if he said anything about it, he knew Georgi and especially Todor would chaff him without mercy.

He walked along as quietly as he could, not wanting to step on a dry branch or into some dead leaves and give himself away to the animals . . . or to the men of Kula, if they were in the woods, too.

Georgi froze. A moment later, Petko and Todor did, too. Ever so slowly and carefully, Georgi set an arrow to his bow. He was the best archer of the three of them—and he'd first seen the partridge on the oak bough ahead. He let fly. The bird tumbled into the brush. All three young men ran up to it, Petko and Todor pounding Georgi on the back.

Before long, Petko bagged a fat hare and then a partridge of his own. Georgi got a rabbit and another partridge, too. The only thing Todor saw was a squirrel, and when he shot at it, he missed. That put him out of temper. He was still fuming, even after the cousins stopped by a little stream to eat a noonday meal of black bread and prunes.

"It's not fair," he grumbled. "You two without six whiskers between you have all the luck, and I—" He stopped and stared. On the far side of the stream, a stag came down to drink. It was within easy bowshot and had not the slightest clue the cousins were anywhere near.

A broad grin spread over Todor's face. He'd seen the stag first. It was his if he could kill it. He nocked an arrow, drew the bowstring back to his cheek. Petko and Georgi sat still, as if carved from stone. Todor loosed the shaft. It flew straight, but too high, and rattled into the bushes behind the stag. The animal's head jerked up in alarm. It bounded away.

Todor cursed God. He cursed Jesus, the Virgin, and all the saints. For good measure, he even cursed the Turks' Muhammad. Then, springing to his feet, he splashed over the stream and ran after the stag, still cursing as he went.

Petko and Georgi looked at each other in dismay. "Your mother told us to stick together," Georgi said.

"She was right, too." Petko heaved himself up. "We'd better go after him. And when we catch up with him, let's knock some sense into his stupid head. Between the two of us, we ought to be able to do it."

"The two of us can beat him, all right," Georgi said. "I don't know if anybody can knock sense into him, though."

Petko laughed, but down deep he agreed with his cousin. He raised his voice: "Here, Todor, wait for us! We'll help you run down that deer."

Todor didn't wait. The sound of his crashing through the brush got fainter and fainter and disappeared. "He wants it all for himself," Georgi said bitterly. "He wants to be a hero, carrying the dressed carcass into the village on his shoulders. 'Little boys with your birds and bunnies,' he'll call us."

That sounded like Todor, sure enough. "We won't let him get away with it," Petko said. He crossed the stream, Georgi right behind him. The water soaked his sandals and cooled his feet.

Todor had got so far ahead of them that they had to track him as if he were an animal they were hunting—and so, in a way, he was. But they had to go slowly and cast about to keep on his trail. He wouldn't answer when they called. "We'll never catch up with him," Georgi said after a while. "He's taking two strides to our one, maybe three."

"We've got to keep trying," Petko said stubbornly.

"I hope that deer gets away," Georgi said. "Then Uncle Bogdan will give him what for."

As the afternoon wore on, that notion appealed more and more to Petko, too. He wondered if, somewhere behind Georgi and him, Todor had killed the stag and was taking it back to Gramada. But then his head came up, like a hunting dog's at a scent. Georgi looked alert, too. They both pointed in the same direction. The thrashing in the bushes had been at the edge of hearing, but it was there.

"He'll be angry at us if he's made the kill," Petko whispered as he and his cousin drifted toward the sound. He chuckled without breath. "He'll be angry at us if he hasn't made the kill, too."

"That's fine," Georgi said. "I'm already angry at him."

A couple of minutes later, Petko held out his arm to bar Georgi's path. Through some thick undergrowth, he'd spotted the dark blue of Todor's tunic. He pointed to it. Georgi nodded. Petko said, "Let's leap out and scare the breeches off him." His cousin grinned and nodded again.

Shouting like wild things, they burst through the bushes and ran toward Todor. Their cousin never moved. The shouts clogged in their throats. Todor lay on his back in a tiny clearing, staring blindly up at the sky. His throat had been cut from ear to ear, as if he were a village hog. Blood, what Petko thought an impossible amount of blood, had poured from Todor and soaked the mossy ground.

Petko and Georgi crossed themselves violently. Even as Petko made the holy sign, though, the rusty smell of his cousin's blood was thick in his nostrils. "The men from Kula," Georgi choked out.

"Yes." Petko wondered why he wasn't more afraid, then found the answer: "They must have done it and run off." He stared at Todor in horrid fascination. He'd never seen a murdered man before. He crossed himself again. "I wish we had some salt to put in his shoes," he muttered.

"To keep his ghost from coming back, you mean?" Georgi asked. Petko nodded. His cousin said, "We'll take him back with us—we'll have to take him back with us. We'll bury him by the church, and Father Boris will pray—"

"That will do for his body," Petko broke in, "but what of his blood? With all the blood here spilled on forest ground, even salt might not be enough to quiet his spirit. And Todor . . . you know what Todor is like—was like. He's just the sort whose blood would take on power of its own, would—would become a Vurkolak."

He had to fight to get the last word out. When he did, he and Georgi both made the sign of the cross once more. No Vurkolak had been seen around Gramada since their grandfathers' days, but the spirits, born of blood, were afterward drawn to blood until they could be frightened away or slain—and what could slay something that was not truly alive?

Getting Todor's body back to the village was a nightmare journey, and night fell before they finished it. Had they borne a different burden, they might have spent that night in the woods. Neither one of them, though, wanted to sleep beside their murdered cousin's corpse.

Men with torches had gone out from the village, looking for them. Shouts rang through the woods when they were found: first shouts of joy, then shouts of pain and fury when the villagers learned what had happened to Todor.

Father Boris prayed over Todor's body all night long, swaying back and forth and chanting in Church Slavonic, which was so different from the language Petko and Georgi used that they could hardly understand. They stayed with the priest till dawn streaked the eastern sky with pink. Then they went back to their houses, got spades, and returned to the churchyard to dig their cousin's grave.

He was laid in it later that morning. His mother wailed over the grave along with the other village women. His father stared with dry, burning eyes toward the northwest, toward Kula. A lot of the men looked in that direction. Some of them, even at the graveside, clutched spears or let their hands rest on the hilts of their knives. Symeon brought his musket to the funeral.

Petko and Georgi looked northwest, too. Petko wanted to avenge his cousin, yes, but he was not thinking of the village from which the murderers had come. In his mind's eye, he saw the clearing where Todor had died, and his lifeblood soaking into the soft, thirsty ground. The hair prickled up on Petko's arms and at the back of his neck. He feared what might rise from that ground in forty days' time. He glanced over at Georgi. By his cousin's face, that fear was in his mind, too.

All through those forty days, the two youths searched the woods for the place where Todor had died. If they could find it, they could bring Father Boris to it. His prayers might make the ground clean again. With luck, the Vurkolak would never be born.

But they had no luck. It was as if the place did not want to be found. Again and again, they thought they were on the right track, only to go astray. "What now?" Georgi asked as they walked back to Gramada, unsuccessful once more. Time was growing short.

"We hope," Petko answered. "We pray." He'd never prayed so much as he had in the weeks since Todor was killed. "Just because a Vurkolak can grow from a murdered man's blood, that doesn't mean it must." He tried to sound confident, reassuring. He failed, even for himself. "We'll soon find out."

He wasn't sure exactly when the forty-day period ended. Work on the farm made him lose the count he'd started to keep. When a couple of hens disappeared from his father's flock, he didn't think much of it. Hens had a way of disappearing. Foxes took them, or ferrets, or even cats sometimes.

Then, a few days later, Georgi was counting the sheep at sunset and came up one short. "I know which one it is, too," he told Petko: "that old gray ewe with the limp on the off hind."

"She never strays," Petko answered, looking out across the meadow. He scratched his head. "They were grazing over there closer to the woods earlier this afternoon. Maybe she did wander in among the trees." It wasn't likely, not with that old ewe, but it was possible. "I'll go look."

He trotted through the grass. It was knee-high where it hadn't been grazed, cropped close where it had. Had the ewe been in a grazed area, he and Georgi would have spotted her right away. He went to the edge of the forest and whistled. She couldn't have gone far.

He whistled again. The sheep did not come. Muttering under his breath, he walked a little farther—and almost strumbled over her carcass. When he did, he shivered all over, like a man with a burning fever. What he felt inside, though, was ice. The ewe lay on her back. Her throat had been slashed, maybe by a knife, maybe by a sharp, sharp claw. The whole scene reminded him eerily of how Todor had lain.

He waved for Georgi. His cousin hurried across the meadow to him. Petko pointed down at the dead sheep. Georgi gasped and made the sign of the cross. He was thinking the same as Petko, then.

But what he said was, "It could have been a wolf."

Petko wanted to nod, to believe what was ordinary, to deny what his eyes showed him. That would have been much more comfortable. He could not make himself do it. "No wolf did this," he said. "It was Todor."

"Todor is dead," Georgi said.

"Todor's body is dead," Petko said. "The Vurkolak, the evil spirit that rose from his blood, is not." He didn't claim the Vurkolak was alive. It wasn't, not really. But it was hungry. He made himself think straight. "Let's get the rest of the sheep back where they're safe—safer, anyhow."

That night, a wolf howled close to Gramada. Waking in the darkness of his room, for a moment Petko did not know where he was. The wolf howled again. He slid out from under his wool blanket and off the straw on which he slept and walked over to the window. He opened the shutter. The window had no glass in it—not even the headman's windows were glazed. A cool night breeze played on his cheeks.

He looked out. The moon was only a couple of days from being full. It spilled pale, milky light over village and surrounding fields. Petko gasped: There sat the wolf, not a hundred yards away. It glared fiercely up at the moon and howled once more. Even in the moonlight, its eyes glowed red as blood.

The wolf stood, almost as if it wanted to leap on the moon and tear out its throat. *As if the moon were a sheep,* Petko thought uneasily. Perhaps that thought betrayed him to the beast—if it was a beast—outside. The wolf's gaze swung toward him. Those blood-red eyes seized his and would not let go.

He tried to look away. He couldn't. He wanted to climb out the window and go to the wolf. He knew what would happen if he did, but he wanted to anyway. He started to climb. His bare foot scraped the rough timber of the wall.

"Aii!" he muttered. Pain broke the Vurkolak's spell. He was able to drag his eyes away from its. It snarled at him, snarled horribly up at the moon, and turned and shrank back into shadow. Petko rubbed his eyes. As it passed out of the moonlight, it seemed to lose its wolfly shape. Just for an instant, he thought he was looking at Todor. Then the Vurkolak reached deeper darkness and disappeared.

Trembling, Petko closed the shutters and got back into bed. He didn't think he would sleep for the rest of the night, but the sun was shining when his mother woke him. He was very quiet as he ate hot barley porridge for breakfast. Afterward, he went out to the well, drew up a bucket of cold water, and splashed it on his face and the back of his neck. He still felt tired, but he thought he could get through the day.

Georgi also seemed subdued. When they were taking the sheep out to the meadow, Petko asked him, "Did you . . . see it last night?"

His cousin nodded. His eyes were wide and frightened. "I tried to go to it. If I hadn't run a splinter into my hand from the window frame—"

"I scraped my foot," Petko broke in. "And did you see it afterward, when it left light for dark?"

Georgi nodded again. "Yes. It was Todor. It's his Vurkolak. We could hope we were wrong before. No longer." He grimaced. "It didn't take us last night. What will it do next, though?"

"Did you see how it hated the moon?" Petko said. "It seems stronger at night. When the moon comes up and it's already starting to be dark—" He and Georgi both looked toward the tree-covered hills east of Gramada. The full moon would rise over them tomorrow, just when the sun was going down on the other side of the sky.

"What can we do?" Georgi whispered.

"Hope we're wrong," Petko answered bleakly, and said, as he had before, "Pray."

Nothing out of the ordinary happened that day, that night, or the next day. Georgi looked hopeful. "Maybe the Vurkolak has gone away," he said.

"Maybe," Petko said. Let his cousin be happy while he could. Who'd ever heard of a Vurkolak going away of its own accord once murder called it into being? Nobody, that was who. Petko guessed it was gathering its strength. He'd been so sure he was right or hoped so much he was wrong.

The two cousins were bringing in the sheep that night when the sun set. Petko didn't like the way the light drained from the sky. It got dark faster than it had any business doing at this time of year. He wondered if his frightened imagination was playing tricks on him. He glanced at Georgi. His cousin's face was drawn. He didn't trust the way the sun was setting, either.

Georgi pointed. A yellow glow showed on the eastern horizon. It wasn't the moon, not yet, but showed where it would soon rise. "Everything looks all right there," Georgi said. Did he want to reassure Petko or himself? Probably both.

Petko started to nod, then stopped. Had a patch of darkness drawn closer to that growing golden glow? In the gathering gloom, he couldn't be sure. He didn't say anything to Georgi. If his cousin didn't notice it, maybe it wasn't there.

Up came the moon, bright and round and shiny as a coin and altogether perfect. Petko's fear left him, washed away by that clear, bright light. His shoulders straightened. His stride got long. All was well in the world.

Then Georgi let out a choked cry and pointed again. Petko had seen it, too. How he wished he hadn't! The patch of darkness, the one he'd tried to pretend wasn't there, had leaped from the ground into the sky after the moon. Against the even background of the night, you could see its shape. Wolf? Dog? Bear? Petko couldn't be sure. Whatever it was, it moved across the sky faster than any natural thing—and its great jaws were open wide.

Those jaws touched the eastern rim of the moon, and it went from brilliant white to black. As Petko watched in horror, the edge of the moon was chewed away. A woman's cry rose from the village. He and Georgi weren't the only ones seeing it, then.

They got the sheep into the pen. Even with the Vurkolak attacking the moon, that had to be done. Only after they barred the gate did they run toward Father Boris's church. Pebbles and dust flew up from under their sandals.

The priest stood in front of the church in his black robe, his hair tied in a bun at the nape of his neck, his beard full and shaggy. "Calm yourselves," he was saying. "These eclipses happen now and again. People say they are the end of the world. But in an hour or two the moon shines as it always has."

"Look in the sky, Father," Petko said. "You can see the dark wolf tearing at the moon. Georgi and I saw it jump up there from the ground. It's the Vurkolak, the spirit that sprang from poor Todor's blood."

Many a priest, firm in his doctrine, would have laughed. Others would have looked quickly and said they saw nothing. Father Boris lifted his face to the heavens and gazed for a long time. Petko glanced at him, then at Georgi. The same doubt was on his cousin's face: Could the priest make his mind deny what his eyes saw?

Almost of itself, Father Boris's hand shaped the sign of the cross. "I see the black thing," he whispered. "What does it mean? What will it do?"

Methodically, the Vurkolak swallowed the moon. Like Father Boris, Petko had seen what were called eclipses. The moon vanished from the sky much more quickly now than he remembered it doing then. When all of it was inside the Vurkolak, it took on a sinister red-brown color, the color of old blood. *The color of Todor's blood*, Petko thought.

"God willing, the moon will soon regain its natural tint," Father Boris said. He tried to sound brave but ended up sounding doubtful.

Higher and higher, the moon rose into the sky. The Vurkolak showed no sign of turning it loose. Two hours passed, three, four, five. No one in the village slept. Everybody stood in the street staring up at the sky.

Midnight neared. The moon remained dark and bloody. Father Boris let out a long, sorrowful sigh. "This is no ordinary eclipse," he said, and turned to Petko. "You had the right of it. The evil spirit means to keep the moon."

"We can't let it do that," Petko said, appalled. "If the Vurkolak won't leave the moon alone, we'll have to frighten it away. That's the way you try to deal with these spirits, isn't it?"

His words swept over the people like a warm breeze driving away night's chill, breaking the spell of fear. Dread and dull acceptance turned to anger and determination. Suddenly, men shook their fists at the heavens. A woman ran into her house and came out with an iron pot. She beat on it with a big wooden spoon. The racket made Petko want to cover his ears.

Up in the sky, the dark shape of the Vurkolak twisted and writhed. "It doesn't like that!" Petko exclaimed. People began to yell and cheer. The Vurkolak jerked again. The woman beat on the pot harder than ever. Others dashed away to get pots of their own.

They alarmed the Vurkolak. Petro could see that much. But the spirit would not let go of the moon. "We need more," Petko said. He turned to Symeon, the headman. "Lord, the biggest noise in the village is—"

"My gun," Symeon finished for him. He clapped Petko on the back, almost knocking him off his feet, then went on in his big bass voice: "Aye, lad, you make good sense. I'll get it."

"And I mine!" his brother, Rossen, exclaimed. If you heard Rossen without Symeon, you could mistake him for his brother. If you heard them together, you understood why Symeon was headman. He led; Rossen followed.

The two brothers hurried to their homes. They were grunting as they came back carrying the heavy matchlocks and powder and sacks of lead bullets. "Used to be you had to rest a gun on a forked pole to shoot it," Symeon said. "This one is lighter than that—but not much."

He and Rossen put powder and ball down their guns' throats, then primed the matchlocks' firing pans with more powder. Then each of them stuck a length of match—cord soaked in some sort of stuff so it would burn slow and steady—in the jaws of the cock. Father Boris brought over a candle and lit Symeon's match, then Rossen's. The two glowed red, like embers— brighter than the moon inside the Vurkolak.

Grunting again, Symeon heaved the gun up to his shoulder and aimed it at the moon. Rossen imitated his brother, right down to that second grunt. Symeon pulled the trigger. The burning match swung down and touched the powder in the pan. Petko heard a tiny hiss as that powder caught. Fire raced to the touchhole. The main charge in the barrel of the gun went off.

Boom! The noise was overpowering, like being caught in the middle of a thunderstorm. Yellow flame spurted from the muzzle of the gun. As women started to shriek, Rossen fired, too. The squeals redoubled. The street filled with a thick cloud of smoke that stank of sulfur—*like hell let loose on earth,* Petko thought nervously.

But the results of those two gunshots—oh, the results were heavenly. Up in the sky, the Vurkolak didn't just twist or jerk. It fled. "Look!" Petko cried. "It's running for the woods!" He pointed to the patch of darkness flying frantically across the sky toward the hills from which it had come.

And the moon! The instant Symeon fired, the instant the Vurkolak fled, the moon was all at once clean and white and pale again, as it should have been. Petko's shout of joy was one among fifty.

Symeon was reloading. After a moment, Rossen followed his lead. When the slow, awkward process was done, they fired toward the hills. "Let the Vurkolak be gone from Gramada forever," Symeon shouted, "or face our guns again!"

The village celebrated the whole night long. For some time afterward, Petko worried lest the Vurkolak were merely biding its time. But when the next full moon sailed through the sky unmolested, he grew sure the evil spirit had left Gramada for good.

Not long after that, Symeon took the yearly tribute of sheep down to the Turks in Vidin. When he returned, his face wore a grim smile. "There were men of Kula in the marketplace at Vidin," he said. "They are troubled in spirit, the men of Kula." He did not sound brokenhearted at that. "Something—maybe a wolf, they say, maybe a bear, maybe an evil spirit—is slaying their sheep and their cattle, too. Whatever it is, they cannot trap it. What a pity, I told them." He went into his house.

No one in Gramada said much, but people nodded, Petko among them. As far as he was concerned, the Vurkolak had found its proper haunt.

~ ~ ~ ~ ~ ~ ~ ~ ~

The Vurkolak is a Bulgarian evil spirit reminiscent of a vampire or a ghoul. It can transform itself into various animal shapes and may attack the sun or moon.

Echoes of Ancient Danger

~~~~~~

Sherwood Smith

I saw the boy again two days after we left Athens. This time he was right on the ship with us.

"Well, we're past the pig island," my sister said, yawning as she turned her back on the flock of islands with their white sands and mysterious sandstone cottages. She hunched a shoulder in the direction of the tour guide who had just finished his talk. "That's it for the gabble," she said, then pointed down the deck past the recliners and the buffet and bar to the pool, sparkling in the sunlight. "Tonight's the dance!"

"Gabble?" I said, looking away from the dark jut of Achaea on the bright green horizon. Fresh, salty air stung my face, and I grinned, loving it.

Alexa leaned on the rail, scrutinizing the new polish on her nails. "Yak. Blab. If I'd known this Mediterranean cruise was going to be so much like two weeks of school—

only with really gross smells—I would've stayed home with Gran."

"We're half Greek. This is our history—our roots."

Alexa tossed her hair back. "Yeah, but I thought it would be, you know, all castles and cool. Like Disneyland, only bigger. I don't think we've seen one thing that isn't broken into a thousand rocks, and then we have to listen to a million-hour lecture about each one." She glanced behind me, then smiled a little. "Well, at least there are some cute boys on this dump of a boat. I just hope they speak English."

She moved toward the buffet, looking over her shoulder again. A moment later I heard footsteps behind me, and a teen-age-boy snicker. The steps passed by in the direction my sister went.

I didn't turn to watch—there was no need to. If there were cute boys on the ship, my sister would find them or they would find her. Fact of life. It was also a fact that no cute boy would take the slightest interest in me.

I looked back at the horizon, but Achaea was now just a faint line. What was next? I wished, as I had just about every day since the trip began, that I knew more history—had read better books or had listened better in school.

I turned away, and that's when I saw him. He stood on the upper deck, smiling faintly, his face angled in my direction. *He couldn't be looking at me,* I thought; boys never do, especially ones like him.

Still, I felt self-conscious as I stepped away from the rail. Then I walked back toward the stateroom I shared with my mother and sister, so I could look at the map again.

But when I sat on my bunk with the now beat-up map spread across my knees, I didn't see the jagged coast of Greece or the thousands of islands. Instead, my mind went back to the first time I saw the boy, on Crete. We were in an old monastery cut into the rocky mountainside. The rest of the tour had gone on, but I stayed behind, standing in the worn spot where the monks had stood for years, looking up at the paintings of faces made nearly a thousand years ago. It was like looking into another world—except it was a world with people like me.

All those saints stared back at me with their broad, flat faces just like mine, and the wide, tilted dark eyes. Then I heard the singing, a distant, echoing rise and fall of men's voices. The melody was weird and compelling—peaceful and sad. It almost made me dizzy, as if I had actually slipped back in time somehow.

I sat down on an old stone bench, and then that boy walked in. For a moment I thought he was one of the monks come alive, but I saw his white shirt and dark trousers, and his long hair, blacker even than mine.

The sense of timelessness disappeared, and I realized I was staring. Feeling stupid and clumsy, I ran out. A moment later the noise and chatter of the tour closed around me again, locking me in modern times.

It happened again at Delphi, when I was leaning on an ancient stone, trying to catch my breath after the long climb. The others were out of sight and hearing. I looked out over the rocky countryside, and this time I heard whispers, scarcely louder than the breeze through the grasses. Again I got that feeling, as if I looked back across thousands of years. . . . If I turned around, the oracle would be there, the priestesses, and the acolytes.

Then I heard footsteps, and there was that boy. His eyes were black, his bones the strong ones of the silent statues that watched across eternity from ancient buildings. Embarrassed to be caught staring again, I shifted my gaze out over the fields. I had just enough time to wonder why I hadn't noticed him with the rest of the tour except at Crete, when he said, "What do you hear?"

He spoke English, but his accent wasn't quite like that of the tour guides and shopkeepers, or like the other tourists who weren't from the United States.

"The wind sounds like whispers—" I started.

It was all the time I had to answer. Alexa called impatiently from below: "Ariadne! Will you hurry up!" She came into sight then, red-faced and annoyed. "If we don't hurry, we won't get back in time for ice cream, and I'm hot!"

I hesitated, turned, saw that I was alone again. So I jumped down off my rock and ran down the hill.

After that I watched for him, but I didn't see him on the gray streets of Athens or even at the Parthenon or Acropolis. We got rain at Marathon and fog at Thermopylae, so I couldn't see much of anything.

But now he was here, on the cruise ship. Would he talk to me again? Or had he found my sister and joined the crowd around her?

The door banged open. Alexa sighed, flinging herself on her bunk. "It's hot! Come on, let's get dressed early, so we can grab a decent table by one of those window thingies. It's going to be boiling tonight, but that French guy said the band is so totally cool that everyone's going to be there."

"I'll just wear what I have on," I said.

Alexa sighed. "Come on, Ari. Don't nerd out on me. I'll get you someone to dance with, I promise, but not if you go in there wearing an old T-shirt and jeans. Where's that blue dress Mom got you? It looks good on you—makes you look longer. Thinner."

She really was sincere. I had to laugh. "Lexa, nothing makes me look longer and thinner. I'm short and square, just like one of those rocks you're sick of looking at."

"Mom says you're a throwback—you look just like those Byzantine people, and those girls on that old pottery in Athens. Maybe the guys here will think you're cute." Her voice changed to wheedling. "Come on, you'll have a good time. Great band, and there'll be lots of guys."

"Does it matter if I go?" I said. "I thought I'd stay here and read instead."

"I can't go alone, and I won't sit with Mom like some baby," she said, looking in the mirror and fluffing out her short tangle of curls. "I want to get close to the band—and a window." She wrinkled her nose. "You can read history stuff—if you're not sick of getting ear-banged every day—at school when we get home."

When we got to the room where they were holding the dance, it was already crowded and superhot. The band had started early. Their music was fast and loud. Some of the kids milled around near the tiny dance floor, watching one another, while the adults crowded near the bar waiting for drinks.

I sat at the table Alex had found until everyone had crammed inside. Mom got involved talking to some other women, and Alexa was already swallowed up in a crowd of kids.

Nowhere in the crowd did I see the guy I'd talked to at Delphi.

I finished the cola I hadn't wanted, then got up. It took me a couple of minutes to make my way to the door, then I was out. The air was cooler by contrast but so soft it felt like silk on my cheeks. The breeze smelled of salt and some kind of tangy flowers.

I moved along the rail, away from the noise and lights. Low clouds drifted overhead, forming mysterious shapes against the stars. Out over the water wisps of fog glowed, ghostly silver against the blackness of an island.

I saw no lights on the island, just faint starlight etching the shape of rocky cliffs. Did anyone live there? Fog wreathed the shoreline, masking everything below the hills.

The breeze was suddenly stronger. I pulled out my braid.

Cool air fingered my scalp and ruffled my hair across my arms. I breathed deeply. The blossom scent was stronger now. I shut my eyes, trying to identify it, then became aware of a faint, far-off sound. At first I thought it was bells, so sweet and clear toned it was.

The amplified thump-thump and guitar-wail of the band made it difficult to hear the bells, so I moved farther from the lit part of the ship, until I stood at the prow.

The sound resolved into a melody sung by voices, long and lilting and sad. Did one of the ship's crew have a radio or boom box? If so, I was going to find out the name of the tape—when I could move again.

My feet seemed rooted to the deck. Leaning against the rail, I stared out over the water, trying hard to follow the melody. It grew stronger, clearer, until I heard three distinct voices, blending with unearthly beauty. The melody changed, larking high up the scale. One of the voices launched into a breathtaking descant—high over my head. The back of my neck tingled when I saw something flicker from one cloud to another.

Rubbing my eyes, I looked harder, wishing for light. Again I saw a flicker: A large bird drifted gracefully just over a distant fogbank, and with a weird swooping feeling inside me I realized that the singers were not on a tape but were live. Close. Yet they were not on the ship.

"Sirens," I breathed, half remembering an old myth.

Only weren't they mermaids? And didn't they do terrible things to sailors?

I looked about quickly. No sailors in sight—no one but me and a boy's silhouette leaning against the rail not far behind me.

"Ariadne," a sweet voice whispered.

"Ariadne," another called in a lovely fall of notes, from high overhead.

"Ariadne," sang the third, from far across the water. "Come, come join us. Come sing with us."

"I can't sing," I whispered, conscious of that listener behind me. And, because the music had stirred up my emotions—and because nothing seemed quite real—I added even more softly, "I can't do much of anything."

"We can give you beauty," came the high voice from above.

"We can teach you magic," sang the middle one.

"We can make you powerful," the low one intoned on a long, shivery note.

All three voices combined again, for a glorious chord: "Ariadne, come join us, and be young for ever and ever and ever."

I leaned out, saw the black sea churning. Fear drove the song out of my head, but a moment later the voices were back again, stronger. Now I could hear words: The melody was quick and exciting; the images the lyrics conjured up were of love and attraction and enchantment.

"You will spin out your own spells," one voice sang sweetly just below the prow.

"Enthrall any man you desire," the high voice promised.

I closed my eyes as I leaned out over the rail, not looking at the black water. Instead I saw myself, not as I was—short, plain, and uninteresting—but surrounded by handsome guys all trying to get my attention. Just like Alexa. But the center of the admiring group was not my sister; it was me.

"Will my life be beautiful?" I whispered, my words almost drowned by the churning waves.

"Beauty, beauty, beauty," the voices echoed softly from sea to clouds.

I leaned out farther, feeling salt-tanged splashes on my cheeks as I saw images of mysterious islands, marble temples, and of dark-eyed people with garlands in their hair and graceful tunics, singing and dancing. And dancing in their midst was me.

Feathers brushed my forehead and arms softly, and the voice whispered on a thrilling note, "You will steal all your sister's lovers and laugh at her tears."

The beautiful images splintered, whipped away by the rising wind. Now I saw myself in the midst of a crowd of loud teenage guys I had nothing in common with, everyone vying for attention.

"That's not beauty; that's just popularity," I said. The sheer disappointment made me smile, and like bubbles rising in a stream the smile turned into a giggle. And then I was holding onto the rail and laughing, my hair buffeting my face and arms in the rising wind.

The voices vanished. I opened my eyes, saw only the last of the clouds drifting away, and behind the ship the black line of an island disappearing over the horizon.

"Thalia summons her sisters," a voice spoke next to me.

I turned around, still snickering, and there was the boy. "Who's Thalia?" I asked. "And for that matter, who are you?"

"I am Glaucus," he said.

"I thought those Sirens did their tricks on men. Or is it just sailors?"

"It's anyone who can hear them," he replied. "In the old days, women did not travel."

"Well it didn't seem to work on you."

He shook his head. "They don't heed me. My labor is to gather the souls they've drowned, until the day Endymion awakens."

"Drowned souls," I repeated, and for the first time I felt the bite of chill in the wind. "Where are you from?" I added slowly. "Or should I ask, when?"

He didn't answer.

A rush of emotions swept through me: relief, curiosity, excitement, and a little fear. Had I somehow slipped back in time to ancient Greece? No—I looked around, saw the rest of the cruise ship, with its modern lights, deck chairs, and I heard the distant thump-thump of the band.

Then the most immediate of the swarm of questions crowding

my brain pushed forward, and I turned angrily to face him. "So you would have just stood there and let me jump over and drown?"

He spread his hands. "But you didn't."

"I almost did," I said. "Until they got to that dumb stuff about taking my sister's boyfriends. I mean, I love my sister, and she is beautiful, but she doesn't see beauty. Those stupid Sirens don't seem to realize that there should be more beauty in the world, not less."

"Beauty without wisdom can be dangerous," Glaucus said. "Few see it. So the Sirens still lure victims."

"But they're gone." I breathed in, shivering in the cold air. Above, clouds gathered. It was going to rain soon. I turned. "And you are also going, then, right? And I suppose I won't remember any of this either," I added bitterly. "This is the twentieth century, after all, and myths don't exist, and the beauties of ancient times are pretty hard to find. Certainly not in Los Angeles, with all the smog and traffic jams and crowded, ugly buildings."

Glaucus said softly, "When the wise don't see beauty, they make it."

"That was certainly true in the past," I replied. "I've learned that by coming here." Raindrops stung my face, my eyes. "Maybe I am a throwback—I guess I belong in the past. There's no magic or mystery now, and not much beauty."

"It is here," he said. "Just as we stand here now." The rain fell faster and faster, and it was difficult to see him. "Listen. See. Feel. And make."

"But I'll have to go home soon," I said. "I don't know if I can ever get back here again. Though I'm going to try."

He lifted a hand. "Some of us dwell in smaller realms," he said. "But Thalia, Clio, and their sisters, they can be heard everywhere—by those who learn to listen for their voices."

Lightning flashed. An enormous volley of thunder made me clap my hands over my ears. When it was over, a hand grasped my arm. "Glaucus?" I gasped.

Light swung before my eyes, almost blinding me, then it steadied: a flashlight, held by a sailor. "A storm is coming," he said, his accent heavy. "You must go inside. Please."

I looked around for Glaucus, but I was alone with the sailor, who tugged me toward the hatchway to the cabins.

Light and noise enfolded me again. People laughing, talking. Somewhere a radio blared, a dissonant counterpoint to the band still playing somewhere above me. Already the memory of my experience seemed unreal.

"It wasn't a dream," I muttered stubbornly as I let myself into our cabin. And despite my wet clothes and cold hands, I went straight to the map and the guidebook I'd bought.

When Alexa came in at last, I was still reading. "Oh, Ari," she exclaimed, throwing herself on her bunk. "You missed a dynamite party. Totally cool music, and the cutest guy from Germany." She rolled over and frowned at me. "How come you just sit around like an old rock? Don't you see how boring that is?"

I thought about the heartbreaking beauty of the Sirens' song and how I'd come very close to throwing myself into the ocean over their false promises. I opened my mouth to tell her about my adventure—to shock and surprise her, make her see me as the interesting one for once.

But as I watched her restless brown eyes, I knew she wouldn't believe me, any more than she'd heard the Sirens sing.

So I looked down at the book instead. "The Muses," I said, not really aware I was speaking. That's who Clio and Thalia were: They were the Muses of history and of comedy, two of nine sisters. I'd just found that page.

Had Glaucus also lied, or would I really hear them? And if I did, what then? Would it change my life? But my life was already changed.

"Music?" Alexa said, looking back over her shoulder at me as she fussed with her hair. "Is that what you said?"

"Close enough." I grinned at her. "The lyre of Orpheus. According to this book, it was good enough to make the Furies weep."

"I'm going to weep if you start talking like those dumb guides," Alexa retorted. "Now, what shall I wear tomorrow? I'm meeting that French guy at nine, and the German guy at lunch."

I shut my eyes, trying to recall the melody the Sirens had sung. Already it was half gone, but I could remember the way I felt when I heard it. Grabbing a piece of stationery from the tiny desk, I started writing down my experience, trying to relive it again on paper.

When I was done, the pain was gone from the memory, leaving only wonder. I looked down at what I'd written. Could I make someone else experience that beauty—without the danger?

Was this the song of the Muses?

I guess I'll find out when Endymion wakes.

Sirens *are creatures from Greek mythology. There were three of them, who lived on an island near Achaea. They were half bird and half woman, and their voices were so beautiful that sailors, hearing them from passing ships, would throw themselves overboard and drown.*

The Bogle in the Base- ment

~~~~~~

Lawrence

Watt-Evans

Mary watched as the movers brought the trunks down the front hall, one by one, and with much grunting and muttering maneuvered them around the corner and down the basement stairs.

She could hear horns beeping out front as the lunch-hour traffic tried to get past the double-parked van, and hoped the cops wouldn't be too quick to ticket it. That would mean an argument between the movers and her parents about who was to pay the fine.

"I can't believe you had all that stuff shipped all the way from Scotland!" she said.

"Well, what else was I going to do with it?" her mother asked. "Great-aunt Margaret left it to me, and I couldn't just throw it all away, could I?"

"Shipping must have cost a *fortune*," Mary said. "What if it's all just junk?"

"It's not just junk," her mother said. "I looked in enough of these trunks to see *that* much."

"You want us to stack 'em?" the man holding the front of the latest trunk asked.

"Not if you can help it," Mary's mother replied.

"Okay," the mover said, and trudged onward.

"How many trunks *are* there?" Mary asked, as the movers dropped the latest and went back for the next.

"Thirteen," her mother replied. "They *should* all fit down there."

Mary tried to imagine how anyone could cram thirteen big, old-fashioned steamer trunks into the little stone-walled cellar of their Boston town house without stacking them. The furnace and the water heater and the boxes of Christmas decorations and the like already half filled it.

When the movers had collected her mother's signature on the necessary paperwork and departed, Mary made her way down the old bare-wood steps to the basement.

The trunks filled almost all the previously available floor space, leaving only two narrow aisles.

"Mind if I look in them?" Mary called upstairs.

"Go ahead," her mother called back.

Mary opened the heavy brass latches on the first one and lifted the lid; inside, neatly folded, were woolens—scarves, blankets, shawls. Mary stroked them and burrowed down into the stacks and found everything wonderfully soft; they were lovely and would be welcome in cold weather, but they weren't very exciting.

The next trunk was full of linens and lace—again, pleasant, but nothing thrilling.

The third trunk was locked. Mary shrugged and went on to the fourth.

By the time her father got home that evening, Mary had rummaged through twelve of the trunks and found a few treasures as well as mountains of boring household goods. She had begged her mother into giving her a carving of a cat, had played with an antique nutcracker, had polished some old brass trivets and other knickknacks, and had marveled at a drawstring bag full of exotic old coins. She had glanced at the books and letters but had not yet read any of them; that could wait.

That locked trunk fascinated her, though; why was just one out of thirteen trunks locked? What treasure was in there that Great-aunt Margaret had thought deserved special treatment?

She brought up the subject at dinner, and her mother didn't know anything about the locked trunk and didn't have the key.

"We'll get it open eventually," she told Mary, "but there's no hurry."

Mary had to be content with that.

Over the next three weeks the contents of the trunks were largely absorbed into the everyday supplies of the family home: Linens went into the sideboard cupboard in the dining room, scarves and mufflers in with the winter coats in the attic cedar closet, and so on. Some items went to the antique shops on Charles Street or to various charities.

The locked trunk stayed locked.

Then one day Mary was rummaging through the trunk where Great-aunt Margaret had stored books and old letters when she happened to pick up a bundle of envelopes and put it to one side.

The bundle had been stored upright, but she placed it on its side, without really looking.

She heard a little click.

She looked and found that a small brass key had fallen out of one of the envelopes.

She stared at it for a moment, then grinned. She picked up the key and studied it.

It sparkled in the light of the two bare lightbulbs that served as the basement's only illumination; being tucked away in an envelope had kept any hint of corrosion from dimming its luster. It was the right size and general shape to be a trunk key.

And there was no better time to try it, she decided. She closed up the trunk of books and letters and sidled along the aisle to the locked one. Half the trunks were empty, but none had been removed yet, so the basement was still crowded and hard to maneuver in.

She knelt and fitted the key in the lock.

It slid in easily but didn't seem to want to turn, and she was beginning to wonder if maybe it went to one of the other trunks after all, when the lock finally yielded and clicked open.

Holding her breath, Mary opened the latches and started to lift the lid.

Before she had it open more than a few inches, though, the lid sprang upward, out of her hands. She yelped and stepped back, colliding with the empty trunk behind her; she lost her balance, swayed, and abruptly sat down on the closed lid.

And there, before her eyes, the lid of the formerly locked trunk was flung up, and a creature lifted itself up from the trunk and stared at her.

Mary shrieked in surprise.

It was black and leathery, with long, bony arms and long, bony fingers, with huge, pointed ears on either side of a mostly bald head. Tangled wisps of white hair clung to each side of its pate, while the center was bare and wrinkled. Its nose was a great dark hook, its mouth broad and lipless, and its eyes a ghastly shade of yellow.

It grinned at Mary, showing a great many large, crooked yellow teeth.

Mary shrieked again.

"Mary?" her mother's voice called from the top of the stairs. "Are you okay?"

"*NO!*" Mary shouted.

Her mother clattered quickly down the stairs, but the thing in the trunk didn't vanish, didn't seem particularly disturbed by the noisy approach; it hoisted itself up out of the open trunk and clambered atop the closed one next to it, squatting with sharp, bony knees thrusting up above its head. It crouched there, blinking at Mary.

Its body was tiny, almost doll-like; its head was the size of a man's; its arms and legs were impossibly long and spidery. Each limb was like muscles stretched taut over bone and wrapped in coarse black leather, utterly without fat or other padding, and each was, Mary estimated, more than a yard long. If the thing stood up, it would be about her own height of five feet two—but more than two-thirds of that would be leg.

It wore a burlap rag wrapped loosely about itself, and she couldn't tell whether it was male or female.

She didn't particularly want to.

Then her mother saw the thing and gasped.

"Oh, my God," she said.

The creature winced.

"It's a Bogle!" Mary's mother said.

"A what?" Mary asked.

"A Bogle," the creature said, sketching a bow. "An' I suppose ye'd hae me gie my name now, arter the fashion o' ye mortals, but I'd no' gie ye power o'er me."

"It talks!" Mary said.

It was undeniable that it spoke, but on the other hand, its Scottish accent was so thick she wasn't sure what it had said. Mary stared.

"What's a Bogle?" she asked.

The creature glanced at Mary's mother. "Are ye tellin' me the lass knows nought o' Bogles? Is she not a McTeague?"

"She's a Fiorelli," Mary's mother replied. "*I* was a McTeague before I got married."

The thing eyed first Mrs. Fiorelli and then Mary suspiciously. "An' this man o' the outlandish name that ye've wed holds not wi' the old tales, then?"

"Neither of us does," Mary's mother said. "Besides, I couldn't remember most of the ones my parents told me. God, I can't believe I'm talking to you!"

"Mother, what's a Bogle?" Mary demanded. She was over her initial fright and beginning to be angry—her mother and the creature were speaking as if she weren't even there!

"*That* is," her mother said, gesturing at the creature. "It's a sort of . . . of Scottish goblin. A nasty kind. The Bogles play tricks on people and catch unwary travelers and make noises in the night. Except I thought they were just stories."

"We're nae just tales," the Bogle added, "we're all o' that you've said, and more besides." It turned and leered at Mary, displaying its yellow teeth. "If you'd hae lied when you said ye'd no' heard o' Bogles, me pretty lass, I'd hae ripped the tongue from your head, for a Bogle can't abide a liar, nor any ither scoundrel or blackguard. That's another thing that we are, it is!"

"Oh, my," Mrs. Fiorelli said, sitting down abruptly on the stairs.

Mary backed away suddenly when she realized that the creature meant its words literally, and that those long, strong arms and fingers probably *could* tear her tongue out. She swallowed.

"Oh, gross," she said. She turned to her mother and said, "Get it out of here!"

"How?" her mother said. "I don't even know how it got in!"

"It was in Great-aunt Margaret's locked trunk!"

"You opened it? Oh, Mary!"

"I found the key in the other trunk," Mary said defensively. "How was *I* supposed to know there was a goblin in there? It's our trunk; I figured we had a right to open it!"

"Aye, you'd the right," the Bogle agreed, "and I thank ye for the doin' of it, lass, for I've been locked inside for many a long year."

"Well, I'm glad you've had a nice time," Mary said, cautiously taking a step closer, "but now climb back in, would you, please?"

"What, and let you lock me in again?" The creature scuttled suddenly farther away from the open trunk. "I'm no' such a fool as that, lass! I'm out, and 'tis out I'll stay!"

"Mom?"

"I don't know, Mary," her mother said, but she rose and approached the Bogle from the other side.

The thing saw that the two women intended to trap it, and let out a shriek of hysterical, grating laughter. Then it scampered wildly away on its long, long legs, springing from trunk-lid to trunk-lid, swinging from beams overhead, bouncing from the ductwork and plumbing as it darted and leaped about the little basement.

For a moment the two humans tried to catch it, but it quickly became obvious that they had no chance of doing so. It danced away, shouting and yelling, whenever they approached, and it was much faster than they were, able to dodge with superhuman speed and agility.

And it shrieked and gibbered constantly.

"Stop that racket!" Mrs. Fiorelli ordered it.

"Ah, nay," it said. "I'm an eighth banshee on my mother's side, and blood will out!" Then it laughed again and jumped over Mary's head.

At last, as it clambered along the pipes above the furnace, at the far end of the basement, Mrs. Fiorelli beckoned to her daughter, and the two hurried up the stairs.

At the top they slammed the door, and Mrs. Fiorelli threw the bolt.

Then they looked at each other.

"Now what?" Mary asked.

"Now we wait for your father to get home," her mother replied.

"Why?" Mary asked.

"Because he's bigger and faster and stronger than we are, and with the three of us working together maybe we can catch that thing!"

"What do we do with it if we catch it?"

"I don't know," Mrs. Fiorelli admitted. "Stuff it back in the trunk, maybe?"

"Sounds good to me."

A gale of inhuman laughter came from the basement just then, followed by several loud thumps.

"What's it *doing* down there?" Mary asked.

"I don't want to know," her mother replied.

They tried to go on about their business, but it wasn't easy; the afternoon was punctuated with screams, giggles, and bumps from the basement. Whenever either of them was just getting settled in front of the TV or reading a magazine, after a lull, there would suddenly come a resounding crash or other loud noise. It was impossible to concentrate on anything.

At last, though, Mary's father walked in the back door.

Just then the Bogle let out an ear-piercing shriek.

"What was *that*?" Mr. Fiorelli said, startled. "It sounded as if it came from the basement."

He turned, and before his wife or daughter could stop him, he slid back the bolt and opened the basement door.

The Bogle, gibbering wildly, sprang up the stairs at him; he stepped back in surprise, and it vaulted neatly over his head, into the kitchen.

There, it snatched up a pair of saucepans and began clanging them together.

"Free!" it shrieked, as it danced around the breakfast table. "Free at last! And 'tis a fine home I've found here! I'll be staying here for long and long, my fine McTeagues! Oh, Margaret McTeague, ye thought you'd seen the last o' me, but your family shan't e'er hae done!"

"My good lord in heaven," Mr. Fiorelli said, backing away. "What's *that?*"

"A Bogle," his wife said. She led him into the living room, where she and Mary tried to explain over the din of clashing cookware.

"They aren't generally so loud as this," Mrs. Fiorelli said, apologetically. "I think it's from being cooped up in that trunk for so long."

"I don't *care* why it's so loud," her husband replied. "I won't have it! I want it out of this house!"

Mary agreed enthusiastically, but her mother hesitated. "You want it loose on the streets of Boston?" she said. "Bogles are supposed to injure or even kill unwary travelers; it'd probably have a fine old time scaring drivers or jumping on people in dark alleys."

"Well, what's it going to do if we *don't* throw it out?" her husband demanded. "I don't want it slitting our throats while we sleep!"

"Oh, they can't do *that,*" his wife assured him. The sound of shattering china interrupted her, but then she continued: "A Bogle can't harm innocent people in their own home. They can harass you, and they'll harm anyone who's lied or killed or betrayed a trust, anything like that, but they don't hurt innocents directly." She hesitated as something in the kitchen crunched. "At least, they aren't supposed to."

"*Listen* to that!" Mr. Fiorelli said. "It's got to *go!* Do you think the insurance is going to cover this?"

Mrs. Fiorelli looked at Mary, who shrugged.

"All right," Mrs. Fiorelli said, "how do we *get* it out?"

"It won't go of its own free will if we open the door?" her husband asked.

"I don't think so."

"Let's try." He marched back into the kitchen to the back door and swung it wide, then turned to face the Bogle, which was crouched atop the refrigerator, watching him intently.

"Here, you," Mr. Fiorelli said, "you can go now. You want to be free? Go ahead!"

"Ah, I'd none of *that!*" the Bogle replied. " 'Tis a fine home I have right here!" It giggled and threw a cracker at him.

Mr. Fiorelli stared at it, frustrated, then closed the door, turned, and marched back to the living room.

"Now what?" he growled.

"Maybe if we ignore it, it'll get bored and go away," Mrs. Fiorelli suggested. "Or at least shut up."

Her husband glowered. "You'd need earplugs to ignore that thing," he growled.

"I have some earplugs in my room," Mary volunteered. "For concerts."

She blinked, opened her mouth, and then closed it again.

"And I have an idea!" she said. "Wait right here!"

She ran upstairs to her room and began rummaging through her dresser; then she snatched up the boom box she'd gotten for Christmas, earplugs, and a couple of tapes.

She ran back downstairs, the boom box bumping her thigh, and handed each of her parents a set of earplugs.

"Here," she said, "you're gonna *need* these!"

"Mary, what . . . ?" her mother began.

Heading for her parents' big stereo, which she ordinarily wasn't supposed to touch, Mary said, "That thing came from rural Scotland, right?" She pressed the power button, and the displays lit up. "And it hasn't been out of that trunk in years? And these creatures mostly live out in lonely, deserted places? Then I'll bet it's used to being the loudest thing around." She slipped a Led Zeppelin tape into the tape deck on the stereo. "Well, around here," she said, slipping in the earplugs, "it's an amateur!"

She hit PLAY and turned the volume to 10. Deafening music roared from the speakers. Mary couldn't hear anything from the kitchen anymore, but she slid another tape into the boom box and cranked that all the way up as well. Then she inched warily down the little hallway and peered into the kitchen.

The bogle was cowering in the sink, hands over its big pointed ears.

"Stop it!" it shrieked, its voice barely audible over the racket from the two stereos.

"No," Mary said. "You get out of our house!" She pointed toward the back door.

The thing leaped from the sink and scampered to the door; it fumbled with the knob, got it open, and stumbled outside.

Mary dashed over and locked the door; then she turned off the boom box.

And when she turned off the living room stereo as well and took out the earplugs, she thought that was the end of it.

It wasn't.

Hours later, when the kitchen had been cleaned up and the three of them were just finishing up a late supper, there came a timid knock at the kitchen door.

The Fiorellis all looked at one another; Mary rose and cautiously peered out through the small barred pane.

"It's the Bogle," she said. "It looks scared."

"Don't let it in!" her father ordered.

"I won't." She unlatched the door and opened it a crack, but kept a foot behind it.

"What do you want?" she demanded.

"Ah, lass, a little peace!" the Bogle said, trembling. "The world's gone mad since I last roamed abroad! Great machines everywhere, roarin' and shriekin', and their stenches foulin' the air, chargin' doon the highways and flyin' overhead, and flashin' lights and shoutin' people and every sort o' noise imaginable brayin' and wailin' aboot."

"It isn't any better in here," Mary said warningly.

"I know, lass—but could ye see your way clear to let me back in me trunk? I swear I'll go back; you can lock me in—'tis cramped, but 'tis better than this world o' yours!"

"I don't know." She looked at her parents.

"Oh, all right," her mother said.

Mary swung the door open, and the Bogle dashed inside, heading straight for the basement.

A minute later it was securely locked in its trunk.

"Maybe we should ship it back to Scotland," Mary suggested, when she returned to the dinner table. "I feel a bit sorry for it."

"Maybe," her mother agreed.

"But on the other hand," Mary said, "I bet no one else around here has a Bogle in the basement!"

(Dedicated to the memory of my grandfather, John Watt, who was raised just outside Dundee.)

A Bogle *is an ill-tempered and mischievous Scottish relative of elves and goblins. Bogles are especially fond of abusing liars and murderers, but they'll waylay travelers or haunt the homes of innocents if that's all that's available.*

Ring-Thane

~~~~~~

Susan Shwartz

The buried ship pitched from side to side as the earth shook. The barrow that held it gaped like a hungry dragon. A spear of sunlight shot into the opened pit.

The deadly light seared my good eye, and I screamed worse than Grendel when Beowulf tore off his arm. My shriek echoed from one end of the barrow to the other. Echoes shook the timbers of the ship and meadhall that were, as they had been, hidden from heaven. I woke from nightmare into endless night.

Overhead, though, in the sunlight, I thought the birds that flew over my ring-giver's gravemound would hear and drop down dead.

Dust and damp filtered down from the rotting wood overhead onto the splendor of Ring-Giver's hoard. The old strings of the harp by my lord's side quivered, then snapped.

My left eye, which grave robbers had pierced, dripped blood. I

105

wiped at it and shambled over to Ring-Giver. My master lay beneath the king's standard he had a right to take with him into forever. The dust had dulled the garnets, each dark as heart's blood, on his shoulder buckles and purse. It spoiled the twisted, buttery gold of his great buckle. It smeared the fierce snarls of the battle-swine on the crest of his helm. And it befouled the face mask—my lord to the life, as far as I could remember. That crafty mask, the work of Weyland, hid the wound that had sliced through half his skull and condemned me to this barrow.

I remember my last day under the sun. Men hauled the ring-prowled ship up from the sea to the burial pit. Amidships, they built Ring-Giver's last meadhall and laid him within, facing the prow. Near him, they set out gleaming gold, the treasure of men, and strewed it with bracken.

Now I am just Guard or Wight, but I had a name in those days. I was the one chosen. No one spoke to me. Two thanes marched me on board. My knees buckled. They forced a cup to my lips, and I drank mead heavy with some drug that made me sleep. Then they left me alone with Ring-Giver and the last torch.

Even in my sleep, I heard men burying the ship in sand and earth and turf—a great barrow that I must guard until world's end. We had all vowed when we sat on the meadbenches never to leave our lord: Now, I never would.

Now, I brushed my fingers over Ring-Giver's helm and his shoulders. His shoulder blades were sharp beneath the tunic with its gold clasps and carefully stitched silk borders from Mikla-gard. She who had sewn them had been a true peace-weaver. She would want me to keep her lord fine, to guard him as if this ship sailed the swanroad in truth, not endless darkness.

Ring-Giver slept on. Not for him the heavy sweetness of drugged mead. I had waked too soon from that drink. I shook under the weight of earth piled into the barrow above me. I could practically feel the sea's waves gnawing the headlands like the fangs of a deathless wolf.

I screamed until my voice cracked and my mouth filled with blood. No one answered; no one would. Then the wanhope, deepest of despairs, seized me.

I watched the torch burn down, loving its light and how it gleamed on gold and garnets. The air in the barrow went foul and thick. The torch guttered to a blue haze, then died in a thin stink of smoke. I couldn't breathe in that dark. I felt myself dying.

As my eyes glazed, corpse-lights glowed and drew near. A last time I screamed. *Something* pierced through the barrow's walls and touched me. And when the *something* left the barrow, it left behind not me, with my hopes and fears, not a man anymore, but only a barrow weight, hated under heaven.

My nature had changed. Now I could pierce earth and wood and stone as a warrior might swim the gannet's bath. I could smell blood from afar. I could cast the war-fetter, the fear that stills and binds, upon those from whom I must protect Ring-Giver or bring to his service.

I set about my tasks: fill the hall; spill the blood; snatch the souls.

Let Ring-Giver rest, his harp and his gold and his drinking-horn beside him, till the giants rose, and the sun went out, and Middle Earth failed. I was his guardian.

Already, I had brought him companions for which his ship set out on that endless sea: those dogs of thieves who lay by the ship's oars; the warriors who had ventured too close to the barrow's east side; and, nearest of all to him, two children. I think they were sons of some thane. They had fallen asleep on the grassy mound and waked me with their heartbeats. I had found them before their mothers could.

And they never stirred, not even when I dressed them in white and put princely armlets and rings on them. The great sword that had changed them lay across their necks.

I alone waked. And that was as it should be. I hunkered

down. Was the hall arrayed? The auroch's horn awaited Ring-Giver's thirst. The gameboard was set, waiting for hearth-companions to play. Ring-Giver's harness shone. And the ship sailed on.

I was barrow wight. I had done well.

~

Thud-*thump.* Thud-*thump!* I woke from deep sleep and crouched, listening.

Paired poundings: footsteps approaching the barrow; one pair quick and hale, the other lagging behind. Starved as Grendel, I heard heartbeats, smelled from afar the blood that coursed in the inner seas of men's bodies.

So long it had been since men had neared my barrow. Men meant danger. When I had snatched the children, *then* I had heard running feet, hearts pounding with fear and rage.

"*Wight! Wight!*" they screamed. They thrust spears into the barrow. One stuck a grave robber, but his blood was long dried.

This fresh sweat and blood maddened me to fight. I managed to take in one new companion, a young thane who stayed on the barrow's slope too long after nightfall.

Thereafter, men walked only on the barrow's west side. Women came not at all, a sore loss for me. Ring-Giver needed a queen to tend his hall, to pour mead and speak fairly to his hearth-companions when we reached the last harbor. I knew I should seek him out a peace-weaver, but I feared those tall ladies with hair like wound gold and eyes like honey and swords. Still, what Ring-Giver needed, he must have. I gathered my craft. . . .

. . . But death came by sea. Again, screams echoed from the headlands. Feet had fled; hearts had hammered—then fallen silent. Blood fell to earth; fire roared to the heavens. It scorched

the turf of the barrow, baked down into earth and sand. I feared
for Ring-Giver and his high-prowed ship, deep in the barrow.
But the fire had died, the screaming faded, and life and light
vanished once more.

In the nameless years since then, I forgot my name and that of
my lord. We were Guard and Ring-Giver.

Then, building began again on the headland: new hall, new
men, new blood.

Who was coming now?

I screamed my challenge. More dust sifted down.

Those paired poundings approached. My unclean husk
sensed the nearness of blood, wet breath. The need for life lured
me up from the barrow.

Perhaps they had brought bread and mead and meat. Perhaps they would eat and drink, then rest. Ohhhh, by all that was
unholy, just let them lie back on my barrow's green turf and look
up into the blue-and-white sky and the terrible bright sun until they
slept.

Then they would be *mine*—new thanes for Ring-Giver. After
sunset, I would climb up to the surface of the mound, drag them
down with me, and change them.

A new sound swirled out. It skirled with the footsteps and the
heartbeats, sweeter than mead, more tempting than the dark.
How long since I had heard music! I was even hungrier for it
than for blood and life.

Music. I looked at Ring-Giver's harp with its broken strings. I
was no scop, no bard with a word-hoard and skill. I lacked craft
to mend its strings. The music wound about me like wires on the
hilt of a sword, forming patterns. Tracing those patterns hurt like
my wounded eye, but I drew closer, the better to hear. Up like a
fell mist, I rose through the barrow.

"And I say that you shall come back to the hall with me, not
throw away your life. Already the sun grows low. Soon it will be
dark, when the wights venture from their barrows."

That voice belonged to a young man. I . . . oh, I could remember how it felt to be that young and to try to sound as if I had more courage and more power than I really did.

The sound that answered the young man made me shake. After a while I remembered what it was. His master was *laughing.*

"You wish to play the harp in a king's hall. I seek a new song to play; and you call that throwing away my life?" The man who spoke was old, though not as old as I. Breath rasped beneath that voice. Age trembled in the heartbeat, thinned the blood. I could almost taste the weakness in the joints that would make him easy prey. But, though the man's body failed him, his voice rang the more boldly. He had the courage and power that the younger man yearned for.

"They say an unclean wight dwells here. Let it find you, and, Widsith though you be, your last voyage will be into the dark!"

"Let me make this song my last and greatest, and then death may take me, life and light together." Again, the old man laughed, trying to win with charm what he might not force.

"You are Widsith, the far-farer, greatest of singers. We cannot spare you." The young man sounded as frightened as any man, waiting for the darkness.

"I am Widsith, the old scop. Take away my means of making songs, and you might as well draw a blade across my throat! You—you are young. Do you not long to unlock your word-hoard and have your lord throw you gold?"

Silence. The young man's heart beat faster. Strong. The lust for glory fired his blood more surely than mead. My hunger welled.

"I seek one last song, Cynewulf, the way your father went out three summers past to fight when he knew he would not return."

"He did not lay hands on himself! The priest said prayers for him!" An old anger rose in the young man's voice. I drew closer, crouching beneath the turf. Would the young man, Cynewulf, strike the old?

These brave fools had *names*, these men. No wonder they were proud. No wonder they quarreled. They had *names*. They even believed in the White Christ.

I pressed closer to the surface. *Let them fight,* I begged the power that had changed me. Never mind waiting till darkness; if they fought, in the twinkling of my unpierced eye, I would leap out, snatch them both inside the barrow, and deal with them at my pleasure. And I would eat their blood and life and *names*.

"Our priest," the old bard Widsith said, as if going over an old argument, "said the prayers over your father because he spent his life like a man. He did not throw it away but judged his risks. As I must. Now, do you go home like a good lad, or do I harry you hence with the flat of my sword against your backside?"

"I'd like to see you try it." Defeat hollowed the young man's voice.

"So would I, my son. So would I." Widsith sighed.

Who would have thought an old man's voice could have that much power? It was different from a king's commands. It did not bid; it persuaded with those rich tones that recalled all I had lost—sun and earth and honor. And my name.

A great singer, in truth; a worthy thane for Ring-Giver.

I was so close to the surface of the barrow that I could see the pattern of clouds and sun—my eye hurt!—flickering across the grassy slope. The younger man was leaving.

Removed from the spell of the old bard's voice, would he obey him? Or would he return with armed men, enemies to let in the light, scatter Ring-Giver's bones, and hurl what was his on the green grass? Would the peace-weavers come too and find the bodies of the littlest ring-thanes? They would cry out then, shrill and grieving, and they would burn me like withered leaves.

Widsith stretched himself out on the barrow. Damn him for a fool—did he *want* me to snatch him?

I listened to the beat of his heart until I could have devoured the entire earth, so hungry it made me. Why had he come here, with his golden voice and his boast of a new song? He would be avenged. And he would be lost, Ring-Giver and I.

Perhaps I could bargain. Master's safety for Widsith's life— what remained of it.

I rose up through the earth and grass, letting myself be heard. Widsith sat up, drawing his breath in sharply. His heartbeats quickened: Despite his resolve, he was afraid, and that gave me power.

As the sun struck me, I could feel the hair on the back of my neck begin to burn. I unleashed the war-fetter. Widsith gasped. I laid hands on him, and he collapsed on the grass. In that instant of his weakness, I snatched him and drew him below the surface of the barrow through earth and wood into the tomb.

I set Widsith down in a place of honor near Ring-Giver and the two children I had taken to serve him and waited for him to recover his senses. The wood of the ship's deck and sides glowed as it rotted, and that must make do as a hearth-fire. Ring-Giver lay splendidly arrayed, and all else was in order in the hall, from buckets for mead to great silver dishes brought from over the sea.

Widsith stirred. Rising to his knees, he brushed up against the two little boys. He ran his hands across the wood on which they lay, then over their faces. When his questing fingers touched the blade that had rested across their necks for so many years, he sighed and signed them with the blessing of the White Christ. Then, cautiously, he rose to his feet. Age had bent and thinned him somewhat, but he was still a tall, proud man. He settled his harp on his shoulder, a gesture as natural to him as a warrior's reaching for his blade.

"A ship beneath the earth?" he murmured. "They towed Scyld's ship out to sea and fired it. But a barrow set on a headland to guard the shore . . . yes . . . that goes very well," he hummed to himself, clearly searching within his word-hoard. "Thus the word-warrior wages battle, bitter war against the barrow wight. Hmmmm . . . no, that's not right."

Abruptly, he turned on me. "Name yourself."

His tone stung me into my first speech, except for screams, for a thousand years.

"Wight . . . urrrr . . . I am Wight. You say Guard."

Already Widsith had begun to move about Ring-Giver's hall, his hands out, touching the standard, the whetstone with the god-carvings on it, the dishes, the coins. His fingers brushed against the men I had brought here, and he nodded.

"No wonder they think this place lies under a curse. Men disappear. Children, too. Christ have mercy—"

"Stop that!" I roared, a sound so horrible that even I was frightened. Dust drifted down onto Widsith's bare head. He shrank back, then drew himself up.

Against my will, I was sorry. In the days when I had my name, I would not have shouted at a man like him. Would not have dared.

"Sing . . . sing to me," I ordered.

He stood fast.

The word came to me, and I brought it out, rusty. "Please."

He reached for his harp, unslung it, then paused. I could smell the terror in his blood and his skin, the terror and the exaltation. How many bards could say that a barrow wight had stolen them and bade them sing? A man could get drunk on that, as drunk as I once got in hall when the loaf-sharer brought the mead around and we boasted of how we would fight our way to lasting fame.

"What will you hear?" he asked, as if I were a man with gold on my arms and a name of my own. "A long tale or a short?"

"We have till world's end," I said. "Sing to me."

Widsith laughed. "I fear that I shall not last that long."

"For as long as you do," I said, "my ring-giver will be worthily served in his hall beneath the earth. Sing!"

I reached for the harp, resting on its skin bag, and handed it to him. Its broken strings trailed fragments of the songs of mourning and praise that Ring-Giver's living thanes had sung as they rode about his barrow. No one had sung of me, nor did I expect it. Until now.

"How long since this wretch, this dweller in darkness, has heard music?" Widsith asked himself. *"Wight ond weard.* Ghost and guard. How long . . . buried alive . . . Christ have mercy . . . that maddens him."

I lurched to my feet, opening my mouth to roar my outrage. How dared he pity me?

Widsith struck the strings of his own harp.

"Hwaet!" he cried, the word that opens the greatest tales. I sank down, my mouth still open to drink in his words.

He sang of his far-farings, the tribes he had seen and the songs he had learned, the lands he had walked, the gold he had won. I beat at my memory. In days gone by, I, too, had had a name and a tribe. I had a ring-giver, still; but I had forgotten his name and his family's line all the way back to Woden— ah, *that* old god's name was one I remembered!

I raised my head. What else, what else?

Widsith played on, his eyes far, far away, his clever fingers surer on the harp strings than those of an accomplished smith, winding wire about a sword's hilt.

Finally, he fell silent.

"Do the names recall anything to you?" he asked as if truly, he cared how I replied.

And, powers of darkness serve me, I growled at him.

"You don't remember," he replied for me. "I ought to name

you Wraecca—Exile, what-have-you. But you do not wander, except when you hunt."

That was when his stomach growled.

There was no food. But I looked about anyhow, hunched over with a feeling I could even put word to: *shame.*

Could I do no better? I had brought Ring-Giver a guest, not just a singer but one of the greatest scops ever to unlock his word-hoard in a king's hall. The guest hungered; but where was the flesh seething in a cauldron, the game roasting on a spit? Where were the brimming meadhorns? Where were the joys of the hall? I had failed Ring-Giver.

Widsith laughed, but not to mock me. "There are times when I am better fed by music than by meat. We can share that at least, if not food. I do not think you need it, being not a living wight but a gaest, a ghost. I have not heard you breathe even once since you brought me here."

I sat, my head down, my wounded eye dripping blood. Widsith looked down. "You know, sooner or later I *will* get hungry, and you will have to decide: Let me go, or change me to . . . into your life." His fine voice grew a little thready. Aha, my fine master, so you are not as brave as you would have me believe?

The thought brought me no comfort. Comfort was for named men, happy under heaven, not a wight in his barrow.

He thrust his harp at me. "Now you sing to *me!*" he demanded.

Thus should men do, I recalled, when they sat on the mead-benches—sing staves of their own to make their lord merry.

But I had no gift, no words . . . and this long beneath the earth, no voice that a man might hear without falling into war-fetter.

Widsith was merciless. "Sing me something!"

"What shall I sing?" He was a ring-lord among singers. I owed him honor.

"Sing me the beginning of all things."

I pushed the harp away, screeched so horribly that even I flinched, thrust myself to my feet, and stood with my horrible pale face against the wall of the earth-grave.

"Your soul is lost?" Widsith's fine voice made each word seem to mourn me. "Let me sing for you, then, just as the cowherd sang before an angel of the Shaper of All." He struck the harp once more and sang.

> Now shall we hallow Heaven's Guard,
> Our Maker's might and his merciful thoughts . . .

Blood red as any gems on my lord's harness dripped from my eyes, the good and the blinded. That was not the weeping of a wound but of a man's grief.

Oh, I remembered now! A shining wight had appeared to the cowherd, who had skulked away from the hall, unable to sing when all others passed the harp. And the creature had said, "Sing me something." And the herdsman had sung.

Let my voice wake the dead. I, too, must sing.

> First of all, he framed for mankind the earth,
> With heaven as its roof, the Holy Shaper;
> Mankind's guard carved out middle earth.

Longing speared a heart I had thought long, long dried up. Sorrow weighed me like gold on a drowning man.

Widsith, though old, was a living man. He breathed; he spoke; he hungered. Soon, he must feast or die—or become like the ones I had brought here. Or like me.

How dared I silence the likes of him—or make him like me, whom even the memory of glory maddened past bearing?

"Leave me!" I screamed. "Take what booty you will, and go!"

Widsith held fast. "Ill luck comes," he mused, "from robbing a barrow. *You* will give me what reward I ask, fairer than rings."

"Get out, get out!" I raved as I recognized what his voice held: the pity of a steadfast heart for the hall, for Ring-Giver surrounded by the thanes who never, never would laugh and hail him. Pity for *me*, lost in the dark.

How dared he pity me? How could I bear it?

I summoned the corpse-lights and thrust my face, foul with tears and blood and death, near his.

"Look at me!" I shouted. "Look at me and hate me before you die!"

In a moment, he would swoon from the war-fetter, and then the change that had made me Wight and Ward, not Warrior, could begin.

And what would he be then? Would he still sing?

I hardened what was left of my heart.

Widsith's warm breath fanned my cheeks, clammy with the bloody tears I had wept. But he did not move. His eyes did not flicker. They were the unmarred blue of a noon sky. But their clouds lay within, and they were dark and thick.

"You're *blind*," I accused. The best singers always were blind. No wonder he had not flinched.

His hands came up, those long-fingered harper's hands with their pads of callus in such different places from a warrior's sword hand. They touched my face, seeing without eyes.

Often a man can escape his fate, if his courage holds and he is not yet marked for death. As Widsith was unmarked. Very simply, he did not consent to terror.

With my own bloody tears, he traced a sign upon my brow.

"*Ego te baptizo . . .* I baptize you . . . ," he intoned. "I baptize you Ring-Thane!"

"Get out!" I cried. I thrust his harp back into his hands. "You have the song you wanted of me. Take anything else you want, but go!"

I had my hands on his shoulders. I pushed at him, pushed him through the barrow's wall. He could not see; the passage through wood and sand and earth would not drive him mad . . . no madder than he already was, at least. Mad and dangerous, more dangerous to me than a troop of men bearing fire and sword against Ring-Giver's tomb, a priest at their head.

Voices rang out to welcome him. Swords clashed; feet hurried—I heard them pounding on the barrow. Men had waited for him, cared for him. I heard them urge him down from the barrow and into safety.

Last of all, I heard him laugh.

"I am an old man," he said. "I fell asleep on the east side of the barrow. And I dreamed . . . I dreamed such a song that, if I never make another, I shall die content."

Assuring him he would outlive them all, they bore him away toward fire, food, and hearth-companions. The silence echoed worse than my fiercest screams.

I emerged from the mound and crouched atop it. I had half a mind to follow them. Like Grendel, I would lurk outside the mead-hall as Widsith sang. I would lurk there and envy them all their kinship, their names.

Wait.

I had a name again.

So? Darkness deeper than Ring-Giver's barrow jeered inside my skull. Grendel was named, and look what a name got him.

Look what his envy and hatred got him.

I was Ring-Thane. Widsith had drawn the White Christ's symbol on my forehead and said holy words, making it so. I burrowed within my barrow as a man might draw his cloak about his ears. Even I, estranged from mankind, could sense that the song was not yet over.

I waited. Finally, I heard footsteps: the young bard, the one named Cynewulf. I held myself ready to spring out and seize him. If he were rash enough to put himself in my power, I would save Widsith from the service of a hothead, while stealing another warrior for my lord.

The stars were faint in the gray sky. Dawn tingled in the air, like feet too near a fire.

I tensed. I could smell the life in Cynewulf, the life and the fear and, yes, the pride. Widsith had wanted to win one last great song from me. Cynewulf sought the first song of his manhood, the one that would mark him as a master fit to succeed the old man when he set out on his last journey.

The footsteps drew closer—on the *west* side of the barrow. Closer and closer. Even if he had the sense to come up on the west, let him come too close, and I would still have him. I could hear his breathing, smell the fear on him. He was half mine already.

From his shaking hand, something as light and fine as the old man's touch when it blessed me fell onto the barrow. I emerged to snatch up whatever had been left me.

Harp strings: strong, new, finely wound. The music they held quivered in them like the blood pounding in Cynewulf's heart. I rose, letting myself be seen against the sky.

I would give him a glimpse of me. If his courage held, why, he had earned his song. But if it failed, Widsith must look elsewhere for his heir.

In the grayness before dawn, Cynewulf drew himself up. He did not wish to flinch at the sight of me; and he did not. He even smiled that he had not failed at the test. Widsith had chosen him well.

Cynewulf raised his harp and voice together.

"Harp strings for you and your lord, Ring-Thane. May you use them well."

Then, by all the powers of darkness *and* light, he saluted me and strode off. I would have thrown him a ring myself, had such been in my gift.

The dawn grew brighter. My eyes ached: the good one and the bad. I sank down into the barrow, the drowsiness of day chaining my limbs. When darkness came again, I would fit the strings of Cynewulf's gift to the harp. I would try . . .

And it might even be that when the seas rose to swallow the earth and Ring-Giver's ship finally set out on its last journey, my songs could bring it to safe harbor.

I said so to Ring-Giver before I slept. Beneath his helmet, his skull smiled.

The barrow wight *was a favorite of J. R. R. Tolkien, who put one in* The Lord of the Rings, *and is derived from Old English (Anglo-Saxon) hauntings. Barrows—burial mounds such as the one in which the Sutton Hoo treasure was found in England—often contained ships and great treasure.*